Candy

S0-ASL-980

*Harlequin
Presents*..

ROSALIND BRETT

love this stranger

HARLEQUIN BOOKS
toronto-winnipeg

This edition © the estate of the late L. D. Warren 1966

Original hard cover edition published
by Mills & Boon Limited

SBN 373-70555-7
Harlequin Presents edition published August 1974

Printed in Canada.

BOOK I

CHAPTER ONE

DAVE did not need to drive in and out of the orange and grapefruit groves. By circling the plantation he could weigh up the condition of the trees and pick out the percentage which would have to be destroyed and replaced. Back there on the grazing land the cattle were in fair shape, and the house would do — when it had had a few more windows knocked into it. One way and another he would have to spend plenty, but it was time his accumulation of cash was used to accomplish his ambition. Further globe-wandering would only eat into it with nothing to show, and he'd had enough of it, anyway. He wanted a home in a decent climate.

The foreman walked back with him to the car. He was a small Afrikaner named Marais, and he was hoping a little desperately that the Englishman would buy the Zinto farm and drag it up from the state of half-rot into which it had slipped since the last owner died. What a relief and a pleasure it would be to work for someone with integrity.

"I've reckoned up values," Dave said. "The next step is a conference with the executors and attorney. Would you like me to telegraph you, Marais?"

"I would, sir. Is there anything you'd like me to get started on?"

Dave's chiselled mouth moved in a smile. "I haven't bought it yet — but I would like to see the lanes cleared between the groves and the roads over the farm evened out."

"The trouble is lack of labourers."

"I know. Let's leave it that if I telegraph I've bought, you'll engage the first fifty boys and get stuck into it right away."

"Thank you, Mr. Paterson." Marais opened the car door. "Did you look in at the store on your way up?"

"The store?" Half in the car, one leg dangling to the dusty track, Dave paused. "You mean the cement and iron building on the corner, as you turn in from the main road? That goes with the estate, doesn't it?"

Marais nodded. "It's actually a trading station, run by a man named Bentley, but he's away on a cruise, getting over an illness. You might take a look at it. The boys spend their wages there."

"Right. I will."

The sedan slid off, leaving a billowing wake of pinkish-grey sand. Dave shifted in his seat for more comfort, and allowed his glance to rove to the right, over the pastures which undulated and disappeared into the foothills of the Witberg mountains. The view through the left window was made up entirely of Valencia orange trees carrying small green fruit, and an irregular patch of molten blue sky. On the other side of the plantation flowed the Zinto River, which irrigated the farm.

It was better than any of the propositions he had so far investigated, and carried ample acreage for experiments. For ten years, in the tropics, he had promised himself something like this. Thirty-three was a pretty good age to start farming, and the fact that the estate was large precluded the possibility of frequent visits from neighbours, which suited Dave's current mood admirably. In South Africa, where native servants were plentiful, a wife was not a necessity.

His mouth twisted with a blend of cynicism and bitterness. It had been unpleasant, to say the least, to land in England just three days after his fiancée had married another man: a blow between the eyes penned on dainty, perfumed notepaper and tucked into a deckle-edged envelope. It was not that he blamed Enid for changing her mind — after all, they had not met for fifteen months and he had always been an unsatisfactory correspondent — but the cow-ardice of her means of confession had disgusted and disillusioned him. Well, all that was ten months away; he had travelled thirty thousand miles since then, and known other women.

A red corrugated-iron roof pushed above a group of wattles, and as he passed, Dave noticed that it was the usual shabby little homestead of these parts. The house must belong to the man Bentley, for only a

6

screen of gums divided it from the beaten earth yard surrounding the native trading store.

Dave stopped the car at the corner of the lane, and sat watching a slim boy in blue cotton slacks and a check shirt. On the back of his whitish curls the lad wore a wide-brimmed straw trilby, and his hands, as they counted the bales of skins and tossed them up to the native who was loading the ox cart, were brown, supple and unusually strong. Veld families ran into big numbers; he was probably one of the Bentley brood.

Dave got out of the car and sauntered over. He spoke to the back of the check shirt.

"Hello, son. Who's running the place while your father's away?"

The young figure straightened and turned with deliberation. In a second Dave had flickered his gaze over the small face and erect shoulders, and absorbed some of the shock. This was no boy.

"I am," she answered. "I saw you drive up the track a couple of hours ago. Are you going to buy the estate?"

"Maybe. Haven't you any brothers?"

"Yes. Two." She turned and spoke quickly in Kaffir to the driver.

"Are they kids like you?" Dave demanded.

For the first time she looked straight at him with a pair of very blue eyes. "No, they're both older, and I'm no kid, either. I'm nineteen."

"Why aren't they here, taking care of things?"

"Because they happen to be in England. One's doing medicine at Liverpool, and the other is taking law in London."

"Good God! No mother?" he asked.

"She went over to see my brothers two years ago, and got killed in an air crash on the way home. I was at school in Grahamstown, but my father's health began to break, so I came home to be with him. If you've any more questions, come inside. I need some coffee."

A self-possessed young person with a way with the natives. Which didn't alter the fact that a trading station in the midst of what was virtually a native

7

reserve was no place for an unprotected girl.

Dave walked through the store behind her. He saw the shelves jammed with mealie meal and beans, salt, sugar and leathery biltong, and was not unaware of the stench of pickled fish and drying goat- and buck-skins.

The girl was already pouring coffee when Dave joined her in the crammed office at the back of the store. She had discarded the straw hat, and the short curls which made her look so young clung all over her head like a silver-gilt helmet.

"You didn't mention your name," she said.

"Dave Paterson, mining engineer from West Africa."

"I'm Tess Bentley." She stirred her coffee, a small anxiety pleating the smooth forehead. "I hope you're not thinking of turning us out?"

"I haven't bought the place yet, but if I do, I shall insist on a man managing this store. Your father must have been mad to leave you in charge."

"No, he was just sick — very sick. I've known most of the families round here since we first came to South Africa, when I was seven. There isn't one who would do me the least harm."

"That's hardly the point. It's the one or two who haven't known you that you have to guard against. Obviously, I couldn't have a girl running a store on my property."

"I don't see why," she returned stubbornly. "I know this business inside out. In any case, I couldn't afford to pay a European to take over for all the time my father will be away."

"Your family has made plenty out of this trading station," he said curtly. "It won't hurt you to drop a few hundred over the next few months."

She sipped at the mug held between her palms. "I expect you're returning at once to the coast to make an offer for the property? Would you give my father the chance of paying for our plot and the buildings on it?"

"I might, but only on condition of there always being a man on the spot."

"I'm as good as a man," she said with sudden

8

passion. "Come back at the week-end and watch me handle a shopful of customers."

"I certainly won't," he said coolly. "Your brothers are a pair of swine to allow a young sister to work for them in such conditions. And you ought to have more pride than to do it!"

Her chin rose, displaying a jaw line of delicate strength. "My father's mad, my brothers are swine and I'm a creature without pride. You seem to have written the Bentleys off rather thoroughly, Mr. Paterson."

"I'm afraid I've never had much respect for people who get rich on the natives' pay."

"We're not rich! I've just told you we can't afford a manager."

"You may not have much ready cash. That's understandable if you keep two grown men in England and another cruising round the world." His mouth twisted with distaste. "I never saw such a sickening set-up in all my life. I'll tell you this. If my offer for Zinto is accepted and you don't put in a manager, I shall go to the court in Parsburg and demand action on the grounds of your being a minor."

Tess took a deep breath and firmed her lips. "You're one of those men who never consider anything except in terms of black and white. I happen to care rather a lot for my father and brothers and if, by taking a few negligible risks, I can keep the business going, I'm not likely to shirk. For your information, Mr. Paterson, my brothers don't know that I'm here alone, and my father was quite satisfied to leave me under the protection of the Mkize family, who have worked loyally for us for ten years. The boy you saw in the shop was one of the Mkize."

Dave stood up. "I remain unconvinced, and the ultimatum stands. Keep in touch with Marais, and if he tells you the estate is definitely passing into my hands, you'd better appoint a manager, quick — because if you don't, I will, and I'll also give your father notice to quit."

She, too, got to her feet. Her shrug was a blend of anger and resignation. "Very well. I suppose it's unwomanly of me to hope you'll break your neck before you reach the coast?"

The beginnings of a smile twitched at Dave's lips.

"Thank you, little one," he said. "I've had spells cast on me before and got through. So long . . . Tess."

She accompanied him no farther than the door of the store, but her hearing registered the series of car noises before he cleared the bend and accelerated. So much for Mr. David Paterson. Tess went back to the office and poured some more coffee.

Her mother had never liked the store, she remembered, yet her ambitions for the boys had kept the family there for twelve years. She had often said that she hoped her sons would remain in England and practise there; that later she and her husband and Tess would go over and settle on the Cornish coast, not far from the village where Tess was born. When her father had cracked up Tess had reminded him of this, but Ned Bentley had lifted his thick shoulders and shaken his head.

"Funny how we all depended on her, Tess. It sounded great, when she used to say it, and we'd have been happy enough doing what she wanted. But you and I don't want it. Not really."

Which was true. Sitting there amid the sacks and rolls of material cluttering the office, Tess realized with clarity that she wished for hardly a thing beyond what she had already. Except for four years at college in Grahamstown, she had had little contact with girls of her own age. Her dresses still hung in her wardrobe, useless now, and it was invariably with a sense of astonishment that she came upon the silver sandals and scarlet slippers among her other shoes in the rack.

Her worst moments had come during the first weeks after her father had sailed. Since hearing that the heart symptoms had not recurred, she had given up worrying and slept like a baby.

Tess liked the Zinto farm. In fact, but for her father's breakdown and the absence of her brothers, she would have besought Ned to try to rent it for the Bentley family. It was a pity about this stiff-necked mining engineer, pure bad luck that a man of his type should be attracted to this corner of the Eastern Cape.

Philosophically, she shouldered off the problem for a while, locked up the store and went to the house to test what Katie had cooked for lunch.

A few days later Piet Marais came to the store. He bought some tobacco and smoked steadily till the bunch of natives had been served to their satisfaction. When Tess came to where he sat on an upturned case, he took his pipe from his mouth and gave a grin which revealed most of his yellowed teeth.

"News for you, Tess. Mr. Paterson's moving in next Thursday."

"Oh." Tess hunched on to the counter, swinging her legs. "How old is your biggest boy, Piet?"

"Jan? He's fifteen."

"Too young, I'm afraid. The new boss says I've got to have a white man here. Know of anyone who'll do?"

Marais shook his mouse-grey head. "You won't get a man for that sort of job unless you offer big money. This is a god-forsaken place to live if you haven't a home or a wife."

"I've a good mind to let Mr. Paterson do his worst," she said gloomily.

"That would be unwise. Remember, he'll be needing labour — I have orders to engage fifty boys at once — and their wages will be spent here. Soon you'll be taking a couple of hundred a month from Zinto, and later even more. That alone should pay for an assistant."

"If it were only money," she began, and left it there. Tess never said anything to accentuate her consciousness of being a woman. Men were hard enough to live among, without that.

Later, she drafted an advertisement for a bilingual assistant, and addressed it to the *Parsburg Examiner*. It was simply a gesture for the benefit of the new owner. Tess was sure it would bring no replies.

CHAPTER TWO

THE Bentley homestead lay back about seventy feet from the track which led up to the farmhouse. In the past six months the garden, which in Mrs. Bentley's time had flamed with colour the whole year round, had begun to disappear into a blanket of weed. The red-hot pokers, succulent bush euphorbias, cassias and honeysuckle pushed out of beds of khaki bush weed, and the acacias and proteas, set just in front of the hedge of wattles and pollard pines, had become threaded with elephant grass.

Inside, the one-storied house had a spare, outmoded atmosphere. The aroma of the whole house was compounded of skins and the paraffin with which Kate Mkize kept down the white ant. The furniture, of hardwood, had been kicked bare of varnish below knee-level by the Bentleys when young. Curtains, cushions and bed covers had faded to a universal drab which was the more depressing because three sides of the house had verandas which shut out much of the daylight.

Sometimes, Tess saw herself ordering drastic alterations. Unfortunately, money was always too tight for the dreams to take solid outline, so she had to make do with jars of flowers all over the place. You could always procure an armful of mountain roses or wild orchids from one of the native women in exchange for a pound or two of meal.

Tess followed the Bentley tradition of living almost entirely on the barter system. She had to, for the bank posted off quarterly allowances to her brothers and complied with her father's telegraphed requests for travellers' cheques; what was left scarcely met the rent and other charges for the store. But so long as they remained solvent she was cheerful. Her father, who had never shared her mother's preference for the two sons, had continually assured her: "You're young yet, Tess, and Zinto isn't a bad place for an adventurous girl to grow up in. Your day will come."

Tess wasn't anxious for the days to pass till her

brothers were independent. In fact, she hadn't a care in the world — till Dave Paterson came to Zinto.

She saw his goods arrive in two closed vans, but the vans had driven away empty before the big sedan showed up. To her dismay the car stopped, and Dave came into the store.

"Good afternoon," he said, and let his grey eyes wander pointedly round the place. "Will you send me some supplies? Flour, sugar, tea, coffee, condiments, dried fruits and anything you've got in tins. A month's supply," he rattled off. "Where's the male assistant?"

She looked up at him in exasperation. "Need you jump on me the second you arrive? I've advertised, but there's hardly been time for replies."

"Sure you haven't had a few and torn them up?"

"Don't you ever trust anyone?"

"Not women," he said, "particularly the kind who masquerade behind slacks and cropped hair. In case you misunderstood me the other day —"

"I didn't," she interrupted. "If I get only one applicant I shall engage him. He'll probably cut my throat and make off with the cash-box, and give you something to think about."

"I've had that in mind, too." Dave lifted a foot to a stool, and leaned his elbow on his knee. "Don't engage anyone without my seeing him first and knocking into him what'll happen if he misbehaves. And I'll also arrange his sleeping quarters."

As he went out he gave her a sharp little smile.

That week-end Tess had five letters; an affectionate note from her father, a few dutiful lines from her elder brother, and three applications for the job she had advertised. Two of the latter were pencilled on scraps of paper, and she flicked them into the wastebox. The third, written in a small pointed script on white bond, she turned about and read twice.

Nothing outstanding about it, except the cleanliness and the scholarly hand. His name was Martin Cramer; he had no Afrikaans but was fluent in Kaffir; he was twenty-six and had come out from England eighteen months ago. Of what he had done during this period he made no mention, but Tess liked his

13

brevity, and was intrigued that an Englishman should consider assisting at a trading station for a small salary. She would invite him along for a talk.

On Thursday afternoon a storm accumulated over the mountains and moved in, a pall of purple flannel. Natives vanished from the roads and paths into the location on the hillside, and a burdened hush settled over the trees. Tess instructed Jacob to close and shutter the store, and walked the path which led to the back of the house. She made a round of the windows, and had reached the last, in the lounge, as the squall arose. Katie was out there, on her way to the family hut on the other side of the hedge.

The first rain came in big lumps which hammered on to the roof. Then, with an explosion of thunder that rocked the house, the skies opened to release torrents upon the thirsting land.

It was so long since Tess had last been imprisoned by the elements that she did not quite know what to do. The bookshelves, having been denuded some time ago for the native school, gaped between piles of old magazines; the gramophone records were chipped and raucous-toned with age; and Katie did the mending of the threadbare sheets and supper cloths.

Sighing a little with boredom, she returned to her bedroom and reached down her dresses from the wardrobe. She could still wriggle into them, but only the pleated tennis shorts and blouse were comfortable. She kept them on, turning about in front of the liver-spotted mirror, her smile reminiscent. It would be pleasant to play tennis again with people of her own age.

It was after seven. Thunder and lightning had moved on, but the rain still thudded like a million devils. That was why the knocking at the front door went on for some time before she heard it. As she paused in the hall, the banging was repeated with such desperate urgency that she plunged forward and released the catch.

What she expected to see, Tess never remembered. Everything else was driven from her mind by the sight of the young man who stood in the porch, streaming from every point of his person.

"I'm sorry to burst in upon you so suddenly," he gasped. "This is Mr. Bentley's house, isn't it?"

"Yes. Come in."

He did, and shed a circle of pools over the floor. "Mr. Bentley's expecting me — Martin Cramer."

"Good lord!" She stared. "What made you come out on a night like this?"

"I didn't. It wasn't raining when I started. D'you think I might slough my jacket?"

"Of course. Let me take it."

"It's too soggy. I'll drop it here."

He shivered, and she became instantly conscious that he did not appear particularly robust. His hair still rained down his neck, and the sports shirt he wore was soaked.

"Come to the bathroom," she said quickly. "I can't offer you a hot bath, but we have plenty of rough towels. You can rub down and get into some of my father's clothes. I'll have a hot meal ready for you in five minutes."

"You're awfully kind."

His gratitude was just a little pathetic. Back in the kitchen, spreading a cloth and drawing the table near to the cooking-stove, she wondered about him. Some men, the Dave Paterson breed, made one feel foolish and painfully young. Martin Cramer appealed to one's instincts. How absurd to be leaping to conclusions about him; she had only seen him for two minutes.

He found his way to the kitchen and stood blinking in the light, a faint, rueful smile on his lips as he held up his arms to show the voluminous misfit of Ned's old suit.

"It's warm, though," he said.

"Come and sit near the stove and have some pie."

She saw now that he was just above middle height, and only remarkable for the length and thickness of his tan-coloured hair. His features were fine and regular, but they had no particular charm till he smiled.

They had started eating when he looked up suddenly, in consternation. "Are you alone here?"

"Yes, I mostly am in the evenings."

"What about your father?"

"He's away for several months. That's why I need an assistant."

"But really . . . I mustn't stay." He was already out of his chair. "Why the blazes didn't I wait till the morning?"

"Listen," she said, indicating the ceiling. "You've got to stay till that stops, so you may as well eat, and we can get our interview over at the same time. Did you come from Parsburg, or beyond?"

He relaxed, and took up his knife and fork again.

"From Parsburg," he told her. "I'd been down to East London, and only got back this afternoon. I found your letter among my mail at the hotel — I thought T. Bentley was a man — and decided to drive straight over. The storm caught me about three miles down from here, so I pulled in, intending to wait till it passed."

She smiled. "Haven't you hit a storm in these parts before?"

"One becomes so used to eternal sunshine and appalling dust," he said apologetically.

"So you sat in your car," she prompted.

"It isn't much of a car. It began to leak, first in one spot and then in another, till I was sitting in a lake. The rain still poured in sheets, but I had to get out and walk, or squat there begging for pneumonia. My own idiotic fault," he finished.

"You're not eating."

He gave up pretence. "I'm sorry. I really ought to be going . . ." He shuddered violently, but managed to struggle upright.

Tess said, "Mr. Cramer!" and the next second was gazing at a slim young man prone upon the floor.

She had scarcely recovered from the shock when Martin opened his eyes.

"I'm afraid," he said quietly, "that I've caught a chill."

Tess slipped an arm under him. "You did rather sit up and beg for it, didn't you? Now . . . can you manage? Lean on me, I'm as strong as a horse. Just through here, to the bedroom."

"I can't be ill here," he said weakly.

"There's no doctor, of course, but I've got some

sulphadiazine which might do till morning."

"You don't know what I mean," he whispered, but attempted no more.

He slumped upon the bed and gave himself up to shivering. She covered him with three blankets, made him swallow the tablets, and left him shut up in her dark bedroom.

The china clock in the kitchen said ten past eight. Tess stood by the littered table, feeling rather helpless. An hour ago she had been alone and very hungry, but now the sight of the cubes of beef-steak congealing in their covering of potatoes and pastry nauseated her.

The Mkize family would accept without question the true explanation of Martin Cramer's presence in the house, and so, Tess thought, would the local farming people when they came to hear of it. No one would contemplate turning away a fellow-being in such circumstances. Then why was she fretting? Dave Paterson, blast him.

Tess decided at that moment to administer white tablets at the correct four-hourly intervals throughout the night, and to watch Martin's temperature. Thank heaven she had the sulphadiazine left over from one of her father's prescriptions.

Next morning Martin was better, but too wan-looking to be allowed up.

"You'll have to take more care of yourself," Tess told him severely. "I can't have a co-manager who acts as crazily as you did yesterday."

"But you can't take me on after that," he protested. "I feel swab enough lying in your bed and causing you endless trouble. I don't deserve to come into your life at all."

This aspect tickled Tess. "You haven't stepped into fairyland, you know. You'll have to live somewhere near here, and there's nothing whatever to do with your leisure, unless you read a great deal."

"What do you do?"

"I kick about," she replied vaguely. "But I've lived here most of my life."

"I wouldn't have any leisure," he said. "You see, I . . . well, I'm a bit of an ethnologist."

17

"You mean you study natives and their tribal characteristics?"

"I didn't intend to sound pompous. Three years ago I was a member of an expedition into Gabon. Physically, it rather wrecked me, but I learned a lot. Back in England I couldn't keep fit, and the doctor recommended somewhere warm and dry."

"So that was how you came to Parsburg," she stated, with the youthful grin. "You'll have to stay in if it ever rains again." She paused, leaning on the back of a chair, regarding him. His longish hair on the pillow and his thin face and throat possessed a grace uncommon in a man, and the faint hollows at his temples made him look vulnerable. Tess had never seen a man like Martin before. She said: "I can't pay you much, but I'd like you to take the job. Actually, you need only seem busy when white folk are about. Katie cooks good food, and we can arrange a decent sleeping place for you."

"I'm not a waif," he said. "Why did you advertise if you can get along without help?"

Frankly she explained, and when she had finished Martin was smiling faintly.

"Your Dave Paterson won't approve of me. I'm not his type."

"We'll see about that! When you're over this we'll go up and present you. He'll be satisfied about one thing, at any rate. He's anxious that I should remain innocent — and I'm sure he'll consider me safe with you."

A swift shadow passed over Martin's face. "May I have a cigarette?" he asked.

"I'll send some in."

Tess hesitated outside the door, aware that her last few words had upset him. She couldn't think why — they had been meant as a compliment. Perhaps he was sensitive about his physique, or perhaps all he really needed was the cigarette.

During the next day or so she learned more about him. His childhood had been a long-drawn mental agony, a tug-of-war between divorced parents. At eighteen he had cut away and taken up journalism, to discover later that he was temperamentally unsuited to the profession. He could write, but interviewing of any kind made him wretched.

The trip to Gabon had offered release and a field of research. Sheer bad luck that he had got sick and ruined his chance of being included in the second expedition.

"Your letter said you'd been in the Union eighteen months," Tess reminded him. "What have you been doing?"

"At first I lived on a farm in the Karoo as a paying guest. Then my money began to dwindle rather alarmingly, so I had to get about and write a few articles for the English press. But I'm not one of those machines who can turn out work at a regular rate. I answered your advertisement because I was barren of ideas and living in hotels costs too much."

"I hope you'll stay till my father comes back."

"I hope so, too," he echoed quietly.

The third morning was a Sunday, and he got up to have late breakfast with Tess on the veranda. In khaki shorts and a white sweater he appeared younger than twenty-six, and his smile had a hint of spontaneous humour. Tess had got into the white shorts and shirt and brushed her hair out of the rough curls and into short, crisp waves, but the breeze soon got among them. Tess could never look slick.

They ate grapefruit and French fried toast, and emptied the coffee-pot. She sighed contentedly and raised her bare feet to the veranda rail.

"D'you think we could turn the lawn into a tennis-court, Martin? It's tough Kikuyu grass, but the weather is mostly too hot for a fast game."

"It could be done. What about a net?"

"The boys could make one of rope and grass thatching. I've two racquets that I used at school."

"I bet you play a good game, with legs like those."

"Too skinny for beauty, I suppose. Still, I haven't really got time to be beautiful, and there's no one to compete with, anyway. But there are some tennis players around, and it'd be fun to have tennis parties at the week-ends." Amazed at herself, Tess went on: "If you like, we can go to the Inchfaun Farm this afternoon. I think you'll enjoy the Arnolds."

"Haven't you forgotten Mr. Paterson?"

"The Big Bad Boss of Zinto? No, I haven't. At least . . ." She stopped to shrug. "It's Sunday. I don't want to think of him."

"You'll have to, Tess," he said firmly, while his eyes turned away over the garden. "I'm not an invalid any more."

"It won't hurt to wait till tomorrow."

"If we do, I'll sleep elsewhere tonight."

The sigh she gave now was less placid. "Have you ever met anyone who makes your scalp tingle and the hairs go up on the back of your neck?"

"Nothing on two legs, but I came across a kudu in the dark once and had those symptoms. I was sure it was a lion."

She nodded sympathetically. "So long as you're prepared," she said, "we may as well go to the farmhouse this morning."

Tess should have got up then, and told Katie to clear the breakfast things. But it was so pleasant to lounge there surrounded by trees, and to watch the lazy waving of scarlet and saffron cannas through the veranda bars, that she slipped deeper into her chair and encouraged Martin to talk about himself. The effect of the gently moving flowers was narcotic, and her lids drooped.

When a car door slammed she mistook it for a sound from the native hut.

Then Martin said: "Wake up, Tess, you have a visitor."

Her lids flicked wide, her legs swung down, and a peculiar tightening of muscle and nerve passed through her body.

"Hello," she said, as Dave took the steps in one go. "What a . . . nice surprise."

"I wonder." The grey stare swept over Martin. "Have we met before?"

"I don't see how you could have. Mar . . . Mr. Cramer has only just arrived," Tess said rapidly.

"I see. A friend of yours. How do you do," he said formally.

Martin began clearly: "Tess has told me about you,

Mr. Paterson. As a matter of fact, we were coming to see you this morning——"

But Tess broke in a little desperately, "Martin, d'you mind if I speak to Mr. Paterson alone?"

He didn't care for the idea, but she looked as he had thought Tess never could look; keyed up and angry, and just a scrap frightened. So he strolled round to the back of the house, leaving her facing Dave across that indisputable breakfast table.

Tess felt the appraising glance as if it were a flame licking over her. Intent upon the breast pocket of his shirt, she said: "Martin Cramer has come to help me at the store. He's English and can speak Kaffir fluently. He doesn't want much salary — in fact he's willing to work for just his keep. He . . . he has to live in a warm, dry climate."

"You did say he was a friend of yours?" Dave queried politely.

"In a way. I . . . I'm anxious to do this for him."

"So anxious that he's got you stammering. How long have you known him?"

"A little while."

"Why won't he take a salary from you?"

"He doesn't need it. He writes for English periodicals."

"You might have mentioned this accommodating young man when we discussed this question before." An instant's pause. "Or weren't you two acquainted then?"

Her head came up, but whatever she was about to fling at him stayed paralysed in her throat. This was the first time she had seen contempt and dislike manifested so completely in one person's countenance.

"When did he come here?" he demanded.

"On Thursday, in the storm. He'd got a chill. I couldn't send him away."

"The rain ended about midnight. You could have let me know . . . at the latest by next morning."

"Once he'd spent the night here I thought that pointless. In any case, you'd have made a fuss and yanked him into other quarters before he was well enough for it. Why do you keep looking at me like that?"

A mask slid down over the jutting features. "Like what?"

"As if every word I've uttered is a lie."

"I'm sorry," he said, not sounding it. "I think I had better have a private talk with this man."

"That isn't necessary," she retorted at once. "I won't have you stamping on his feelings as you stamp on mine. You've seen that he's genuine. He can sleep in the rondavel at the end of the garden and take his meals here at the house. You've got what you ordered — a man at the store — and now you can leave us both in peace."

"You're either terribly young," he answered with cold sarcasm, "or the typical product of a shiftless family. In spite of you, I mean to speak plainly to Mr. Cramer, and to insist that he lodge with Marais, at the foreman's house. Tell him to come up before lunch and to bring his belongings."

Some moments had to pass before Tess could reply. She was breathing unevenly as she said. "You probably had a reason for coming here this morning, Mr. Paterson?"

"Yes, I did — a social one, but my appetite for the pleasanter side of life seems to have dried up."

He turned and left her, strode down the path and out of the gateway with infuriating arrogance.

The new arrangement worked satisfactorily. Martin settled into the spare bedroom at the rambling Marais bungalow, but spent most of his waking hours at the store or in the Bentley house.

Martin brought down titbits of news. Dave was working hard to recondition the citrus, and he had started a fine nursery of seedlings. The cattle were being injected against this and that disease, and the far acres were cleared for new planting. Marais had said that a house-warming party was in the air.

"House-warming?" Tess echoed. "I can't believe it. Who is he inviting?"

"The farmers, and people he knows in Parsburg. I expect he'll ask you, too."

"I wish he would, to give me the pleasure of refusing. Have you been into the house yet, Martin?"

"Once, a week ago. I was going back in the even-

22

ing and he had to jolt along behind my bus. When I stopped, he told me to change cars and go up for a sundowner."

"I hope you were suitably abject."

He laughed. "I'll confess I m glad he's not my boss. I got the impression that only geniuses should get their work published, and that all other writers are superfluous. But he told me some good yarns about the Gold Coast. Sounded as if he'd like to go back to the tropics."

"I wish to heaven he would!" she said sincerely.

But now that he had accepted Martin, Dave made no trouble for the store.

If Tess happened to be within view when he passed on his way to town, he nodded amicably but never stopped, which suited her very well. When news trickled through that the house party up at the farm had been a great success, she merely shrugged. One doesn't hobnob socially with one's grocer; at least, men like Dave Paterson didn't. Ah well, she was quite content with Martin's companionship. No snobbery about him.

They had formed the habit of having a knock-about game of tennis every Sunday morning, lunching together, and driving to the river in the afternoon. Tess often had an urge to slide into the cool water, but she never mentioned this to Martin. Possibly it wasn't safe for him to bathe.

One Sunday he brought along a book of obscure-sounding verse and read to her. He lay with one hand under his head and the other lodging the small volume on his chest, while Tess sat with her back to a tree-trunk, hearing his expressive voice without dissecting the words.

Even out of the sun the air vibrated with heat, and scarcely an insect stirred in the grass, nor a bird in the trees. Martin's tones melted into the lazy gurgle of the river. Abstractedly, Tess watched the movements of his lips and the pleating of his forehead.

"You're not listening," he accused her.

"I am — to your voice. The meaning is too wrapped up for a hot Sunday afternoon. We had a large lunch."

"You did," he teased, flinging the book aside. "You're of the earth, Tess. A greedy, graceful sapling. It's a happy thing to be."

"Are you glad you came here?"

"I can't tell you how glad." He cast a swift smiling glance up at her. "I never found writing so easy before, nor such an abundance of material — and I enjoy the store, smells and all. But you're what I'm really grateful for."

"I? You've just acknowledged that my feet are firmly planted and I haven't a soul above vittles."

"That's why. You're so sound, Tess." He raised himself on his elbow, twisted, and rested his head in her lap. "You don't mind?"

"Not if you don't. My slacks probably reek of paraffin."

"A bit. But I prefer paraffin on you to Chanel on some other girl." He settled more comfortably. "I'd like to sketch you from this angle. You wouldn't recognize yourself."

"You're taking an unfair advantage."

"That's all you know about it. Why do you keep your hair so short, Tess? It's lovely, but why?"

"Katie's cut it for me ever since I was a kid. Let's talk about something more thrilling.

His smile faded and the bluish lids half-closed over his eyes. "To me, nothing more thrilling exists. I'm falling in love with you."

Tess had to pause before she could laugh. "Is it pleasant?"

"It would be, if there were any hope of your marrying me."

"Marriage is stodgy. It seems a pity that the excitement of falling in love should so often end that way."

Martin's mouth narrowed. "I shall never ask you to marry me. You deserve someone better than a crock and a half-baked journalist." His face turned into her waist, his hand found hers and gripped. "I've never loved anyone, Tess — never been loved. This is new, and painful."

For a change she had no reply handy. An unfamiliar little ache had started just below her throat, and she fought away from it. For a man he was so dreadfully sensitive.

"I'd make a rotten wife," she said huskily. "Give me a cigarette, Martin."

He waited a minute, then dragged himself up to sit beside her. His smile, as he hollowed his hand round the lighter, was tight.

Quietly, he asked, "You won't let it make any difference, will you, Tess?"

"Of course not." But she knew, as well as he, that a thing once said is said for ever.

The following Saturday they went to supper at Inchfaun. Martin had met Everard and Cath Arnold up at the farm, and in their usual hospitable fashion they had insisted that he must soon come over for a meal and a chat. His explanation that he was working with Tess at the store had delighted them.

"Grand!" Cath had exclaimed in her large way. "Make Tess come with you. It's time she grew up."

That Thursday, it being the day when the Arnolds' monthly supplies were delivered, Tess sent up a note, and Jacob brought it back, scribbled over the margin with, *You're both welcome, Tess, and bring your guitar!*

For nearly a year Tess had forgotten her guitar. At lunch-time she turned out the cupboard in her room and found it, dusty, rather smaller than she remembered it, with two strings missing. She cleaned it, rootled out some strings from old stock at the store, and spent a blissful hour tuning up and practising.

So, at six on Saturday evening, Martin, Tess, in slim-fitting blue linen, and the resurrected guitar, arrived at Inchfaun Dairy Farm, and were inclusively greeted by the bluff Everard and his wife. Hazel, the small Arnold daughter, slept peacefully in her back bedroom.

They ate beef hash with pumpkin, and a pineapple salad, and afterwards Cath played the twangy little piano, Tess pinged at the guitar and the men sang.

It was later, in the kitchen, when Tess was helping to prepare savouries to accompany the nightcaps, that Cath mentioned Dave Paterson.

"He's likeable when you get to know him. We forced ourselves upon him in our usual steam-roller fashion and more or less compelled him to give a house-warming. It was quite a binge — at least thirty guests — and he was a charming host. There were younger folk than you there, Tess. Why didn't you go?"

"I wasn't invited." Tess sounded just a trifle smug. "We don't care for each other."

Cath smiled. "He does show a preference for married women, but I expect it's only temporary. A man of his age and looks is sure to have had plenty of experience."

"Too much." Tess deftly sliced a hard-boiled egg. "I'd pity the woman who married him. Once she'd changed her name to his she wouldn't have a thing to call her own."

Cath laughed outright, and began setting out biscuits and toast-fingers. "I don't wonder you two are enemies," she said cryptically. "You've so much in common."

CHAPTER THREE

MARTIN had been asked by his agent to try a short story with native characters. The letter had hinted at a market for a book of such tales once his name had appeared in good magazines. Uplifted, he had conned over his notes, found them insufficient, and straightway begged an old native customer to allow him to do some prying in his village, which lay in a valley of the Witberg foothills. It was arranged that he go there bearing sweets, tobacco and a few hair ornaments, and prepared to listen to the elders without making notes. To write while the old men of the village ransacked their memories would be in the worst possible taste.

"I'll go with you," Tess had offered. "What you let slip I may pick up."

It was dusk before they got away, waved off by

the entire grinning village. Both Martin and the natives had spent a profitable afternoon.

Martin never stayed at the house with Tess after dark. Before they parted he asked if he might work most of tomorrow in her lounge, where it was cool and quiet.

So Tess did not wear her tennis kit on Sunday morning. She compromised with navy shorts and a clean white shirt, and decided to do some gardening. But the garden was large, the weeds legion, and she perspired. She drank grenadilla and took some to Martin, but though he broke off from his work she could tell that the disturbance was unwelcome.

So she collected his glass, went to her bedroom for her swim-suit, got into Martin's car, and racketed along the road to their usual spot by the river. The water had lowered, leaving a short silt bank on either side, but it still ran clear and fresh, a benediction as it lapped over her body and cooled her scalp.

Tess twisted on to her front, found her feet, waded over to the other bank and heaved herself up on to the grass. Critically she walked from tree to tree, occasionally pressing at a bright orange and finally selecting a couple of navels. She returned to the bank and sat down, her legs dangling over the shallow water.

There were sounds back in the trees; a dog's growl, and then a man's shout, "Seize 'em, Carlo!"

Swiftly, Tess turned her head. She saw the wide jaws and stretched underpart of an Alsatian, felt the dog's impact and shot headlong into the river. The dog was on her, treading her below the surface and snapping round her face and neck. A spear stabbed her nape, and terror stopped her breathing, but her arms still flailed, punching the beast's head and swinging at the heavy paws that pinned her. Oh God, the great brute was . . . killing her.

She didn't know the details of what happened next, but in a minute or so the dog was gone and a man was lifting her to the bank. Her breath returned in terrible sobbing gasps against his chest, and scalding tears chased down her face. She could not see the blood gushing from her wound over Dave's wrist, but she could feel the hot, dragging pain which intensified with every drawn breath.

"You did it," she panted. "You set that hound on me. Leave go of me, you beast. Leave go!"

She pummelled him as she had punched at the Alsatian, with doubled fists and a frenzy of strength.

"Stop it!" he commanded, still holding her tight.

"I won't!" She scarcely realized that she was screaming. "You saw me sitting there eating one of your rotten oranges and you made the dog go for me. I heard you, I tell you. I heard you!"

"Will you shut up," he bit out, "and for God's sake stop struggling, or I'll knock you out."

"Take your filthy hands away!"

Her nails dug fiercely into his bicep and he dropped his arm. She swayed back, her eyes dilated at the red pool and runnels over his knuckles and forearm.

A muscle jerked in his jaw. "That's your blood, and if you carry on like this you'll lose more," he said grimly. "I'm going to take you to my house."

"No," she answered dazedly. "My things are the . . . other side of the river. I'll swim across . . . and drive home."

"It's my guess and earnest hope that in a few seconds you'll collapse in a dead faint."

"I never . . . fainted in my life."

Her fingers went up over her eyes, slid through her wet hair, and she reeled. David slipped both arms under her and carried her through the trees to his car. He put her in the back, pulled off his shirt, folded it and carefully inserted it under her shoulders, and went round to the driving-seat.

The next half-hour passed in a series of nightmares. She lay in a bedroom and had to swallow tablets. The torn flesh was soaked with something searing and dressed. She drank a horrible draught from a glass, was covered and left to sleep.

When she awoke Dave was there, reading a newspaper. He dropped it to the floor and came over.

"Don't move till you're wide awake. It may hurt."

She knew better than to ignore the advice, but as soon as she had him focused and the immaculate room had steadied itself, she rose cautiously on her elbow.

"I'm going home," she said dully.

"All in good time. I sent a boy for Cramer's car and your things—a white shirt and some pants. He couldn't find anything else."

"That's all I had."

"No shoes?"

"No. May I have the clothes?"

He brought them from a chair. "I've slit the shirt right down the front so that you'll get into it easily. Here, let me help."

"Damn you," she muttered, clutching it against her. "Get out."

He stood over her, his mouth thinning into an angry smile. "You're blaming me for this morning's incident. Do I strike you as the sort of man who'd set a dog on a girl? Since the citrus started to ripen we've had natives from over the river haunting the bank. I've been training the dog to scare them. I heard a noise and sent him, that was all. How the hell was I to know you bathed there?"

Her hair, dry now and tousled, fell forward in a rough wave over her eyes. Her tongue came out to moisten her lips. "I shan't . . . any more. Please go."

The defeat in her tone subtly changed the atmosphere. She said nothing when he drew the short sleeves over her arms and turned back the blanket so that she could push her feet into the shorts. His hold, as he assisted her to the floor, was firm and gentle, and he closed the zipper at her waist as if it were a duty performed with the ease of regularity.

"There, you're a boy again," he said. "I'm just as relieved as you are."

Tess could not smile. Her neck held stiffly, she walked round the bed to the door, grasped its edge for a moment and passed into the corridor with Dave at her side.

"Before you leave you must have some warm milk and toast," he told her. "It's nearly five o'clock and you've had no lunch."

Her voice cracked. "I want to go. Can't you understand? I want to go home and be alone!"

They had reached the panelled hall. He faced her, but apparently deemed it wiser not to touch her.

"Look, Tess. I can't apologize for what happened this morning — it's too big. I've spent the whole day cursing myself and that blasted dog. I'd rather the Africans had stripped every tree on the estate than have risked such a thing. I know what it is that's upsetting you . . ."

"You don't."

"I believe I do. For five minutes you did everything you despise in a woman. You clung to a man and cried, you lost control and practically passed out—and worst of all, the man was me. What you fail to realize is that a boy of your age wouldn't have reacted much differently in those circumstances. You've nothing to be ashamed of."

"You mean I've nothing to be proud of." Her lips trembled and she blinked rapidly. "If you're really anxious to do what's best for me, take me home . . . now."

He gave a brief sigh. "Sit down till I've brought the car round."

Dave went with her as far as the steps of the house. "Don't forget the hot milk, I'll come down tomorrow to see if the dressing needs renewing."

"You needn't bother. Martin can do it for me."

"I'll come just the same, and it hadn't better be tampered with before I see it. Is your servant there to help you?"

"Yes," she replied wearily.

"Go along in, then, and get to bed. And let the rest of those tears out of your system. So long."

Next morning Martin came early and called first at the house. Tess was up but still pale and heavy-eyed, and his worried enquiries made her edgy.

"I'm sorry to be like this," she said. "It'll wear off. Jacob took the store keys. I'll come down later."

"You stay here, Tess," He paused. "I told Paterson he ought to have shot the Alsatian."

"What good would that do? He only obeyed his master. I was in the wrong, and paid for it."

"The episode shook Paterson."

"Not so much as it shook me. How did you get on with your writing yesterday?"

"I can't trouble with it while you're sick. Everything

else has become so unimportant. I'll never let you go off alone again."

"Let's forget it," she said abruptly.

She had a sudden longing to escape, though she was not quite sure from what. She only knew that Dave Paterson had so spoiled her delight in an unflurried existence that its charms were in danger of disintegration. The only way to handle the situation was with her usual insouciance. At nine o'clock she walked over to the store and checked over with Martin some goods which had been delivered last Friday.

It was just gone ten when Dave came in. He addressed Martin in a cold, clipped voice.

"You undertook to run this place on your own for a while. That's what you're here for — to take charge when necessary."

Tess came round the counter, a smooth smile on her lips. "Good morning, Mr. Paterson. Can we sell you something?"

"I'll talk to you over at the house."

He stood aside. She shrugged and preceded him out into the sunshine.

As they crossed the yard she said, "At your age you should have learned that it's bad psychology to call down another man in front of a woman."

"So you're a woman today," he replied with irony. "That helps to clear the air. How does the neck feel?"

"Normal. I'd forgotten it."

"Cut out the bravado and tell me the truth."

"The truth, Mr. Paterson," she returned blandly as they reached the veranda, "is that I'd rather die of rabies than allow you to touch it. Will you have a drink?"

"No, thanks." He sat on the grass table, his regard disconcertingly shrewd upon her face. Unexpectedly he asked, "Heard from your father lately?"

"I had an airmail last week."

"Where is he?"

"In South America."

"That's fine. He'll probably bring you home a Spanish stepmother, and you can work to keep her, too. How are the lordly brothers getting on?"

"What do you care?"

31

"I don't," he said crisply, "but I'd like to meet them, just once. Even Cramer is worth a dozen such relatives as you seem to possess."

"You're very kind to Martin." She leaned farther back in the wicker chair and crossed her ankles. "You ought to have a domineering wife and six brats, Mr. Paterson. They'd keep you out of other people's affairs. It's easy to see why you're not married."

"Yes?" with mockery.

"Yes," she echoed flatly. "You can't fall in love because you suspect everyone. And though it's said that women like to be mastered, beyond a certain point the very masculine man repels them."

"It may surprise you to hear that I was once engaged."

"It does." Her brows lifted. "She had a lucky escape."

Softly, he said: "If you're trying to annoy me, Teresa, you're not succeeding. Once before when I came in friendly spirit your pigheadedness put me off. It won't this time, because I recognize your obstinacy for what it is—a natural wall of defence."

"You don't have to be matey just because your dog pushed me in the river. I'm no more worth knowing now than I was a month ago."

He grinned. "Did I once say you had no pride? I take it back. The Arnolds and a few others are coming to my place to dinner next Saturday. Will you come, too?"

"No!"

"You've been to Inchfaun, and Zinto is much nearer. Will you come if I include Cramer?"

Tess got out her handkerchief and dabbed at the corners of her mouth. Watching her, his cynicism vanished. He straightened and spoke quietly.

"You must get tired of acting tough. I didn't intend to say this now—I hoped we'd understand each other first, but you won't have it. I'm going to write to your father through my lawyer, giving him notice to quit."

Her handkerchief slipped to the floor, and her fingers fastened over the arms of her chair. A lost look came into her blue staring eyes.

"You're . . . kicking us out?"

He became intent upon the garden, and his manner took a sharp, impersonal note.

"Until yesterday I'd thought the present arrangement could continue till your father returns. While you were asleep in my room I came down to see Cramer, and from the way he took the news that you were hurt I guessed that he's in love with you."

"How does that affect the store?"

"The place belongs to me, and I just won't tolerate that kind of thing." Almost irritably he went on: "If he were an ordinary healthy sort of fellow I'd encourage you to marry him and take a long lease on the store. But he's a misfit, neither a real writer nor a good trader."

"Martin's never had a chance, but he's happier here than he has ever been, and he is writing well. Every article he writes here is accepted."

Dave wheeled and looked at her. "Does he mean much to you?"

"Quite a bit. If only . . ." She pushed on the chair arms and stood up ."It's no use, if you've decided."

"If only what? You might as well finish."

"Well . . . Martin can't write without encouragement and the knowledge that he's needed. Working at the store and contact with me are changing him. Only a few days ago he had a letter congratulating him and asking for a particular type of story and I think he's certain to turn out some excellent stuff—so long as he isn't jerked out of these surroundings."

"My . . . God," he said, on a long-drawn, incredulous note. "You can't be taking on still another man." He came close, his eyes searching into hers. "You're the most extraordinary creature I've struck. Don't you ever think about yourself—pretty clothes and good times, and the feelings deep inside you? Could Martin satisfy your woman's needs? You're crazy."

Tess couldn't believe that it was Dave's hands holding her face. Dave's mouth hard and warm upon her own. And she was completely unaware that the pulsing beneath her fingers came through Dave's ribs from his heart.

When he let her go she gazed at him like a child at a problem picture.

"That," he said in an odd tone, "is an experience which will do you more good than it will do me. It should prove a working sample if Martin ever gets busy."

She saw him stride down the path and leave the gate swinging. And, strangely, she touched not her burning lips but the nape of her neck, where pressure had started a new spurt of blood to stain the dressing.

Days passed, the wound healed and Martin began to smile again. Tess reproached herself for neglecting his feelings and invited him to work in the lounge the whole of the next week-end.

She wondered if Dave had carried out his threat or postponed the decision for a while. Like the rest of the growers at this season, he was becoming intensely busy. On the far side of his plantation picking had begun. Tess saw his lorry loaded with lug-boxes pass the store two or three times a day.

"The boys keep whispering about liquor," Martin said. "Did your father supply them?"

"We're not licensed, but we've always ordered a few cases around autumn. I daren't do it this year."

"Paterson?"

Tess nodded. "It's a pity. We made very little on it, but the people got a kick out of affording a couple of bottles once a year. It was a change from their home-made brew, and made them feel good and expansive."

Inevitably, Martin was caught and bound by the simple directness, the clean limbs and tensile body, and the unsullied blue eyes of Tess Bentley. Her courage and nonchalance in a universe packed tight with terrors made him humble; her faintly antiseptic scent from the soap she used accentuated for him her innocence and need for protection; her sweet curves he admitted wryly, unbearably quickened his blood. This last was one of the reasons he worked so unstintingly at his writing; he hadn't the physical outlet for frustrated emotion of the sportsman or athlete. The other reason was founded on fear and hope: in a few weeks he was due for another overhaul by the specialist in Johannesburg.

Early one evening, loitering on the Bentley veranda

after the store was closed, he told Tess about it.

"I shouldn't be gone long—not more than four days, and I'll fix it to take in a week-end."

"You're excited about it, Martin." In the softening light her mouth was tender. "When do you go?"

"Not for a couple of months — in August. But I've a hunch the doctor will give me good news. I've never felt so alive."

"No one has chest trouble in this district. I don't see why you shouldn't stay on after my father returns, even if it's only as a boarder with Piet Marais."

His hand slipped along the veranda rail, to cover hers. "I hope you'll want me to stay, Tess."

"Of course I shall."

His smile was a little tense. "Tess, if . . . supposing this chap's satisfied with my bellows, would you . . ." He stopped, flushing. "It's lousy of me to try to drag a half-promise out of you. You see, you're the most wonderful thing that ever came into my life. Don't blame me for wanting to cling to it."

Tess was moved. She smiled and twisted her hand to clasp his. "I'll always be somewhere about, Martin."

He smoothed out her fingers and pressed them to his cheek. "Good night," he whispered, and was gone.

It was for Martin's sake that she went more often to Inchfaun. Cath Arnold's pretty cousin, Mariella Carr, had come up from the coast for a long vacation, and Cath had declared an open invitation to all who cared to make the evenings bright for the dark-haired, merry young lady.

In order to compete with the holiday-minded Mariella, Tess had had to buy a couple of gay dresses and some new white sandals. Compared with the older girl's magnolia bloom, Tess was a budding tea-rose. Here in the backveld, Mariella's allure faintly shocked the women and unsettled the young men. The only man who seemed thoroughly at home with her, Tess noticed, was Dave Paterson.

Tess had not known that he was to be of the party that evening. She and Martin had arrived too late for supper, and had eaten some sandwiches and fruit in Cath's kitchen before joining the guests who danced and chattered between the lounge and veranda. The piano, played by a grave man in glasses, emitted rhythm but little music, for it was old and needed tuning.

"Shall we dance?" said Martin.

Tess patted the pearls over the high neckline of her blue dress and raised her slim tanned arms. Martin's hold always began light and reverent, but the brush of her hair against his skin and the supple ease of her body close to his invariably tightened his sinews. He was downcast yet glad when, as the pianist faded out, she suggested a rest on the veranda.

They found an unoccupied wicker bench and stayed there, saying little till a gramophone started up and the veranda emptied.

"Dance again?" asked Martin.

Tess shelved her own inclinations and smilingly said no. She was on the point of starting him off on a description of his latest story when Dave came out of the house with Mariella, and escorted her down the steps into the sprawling, wooded garden.

"Wasn't that Paterson?" enquired Martin from her other side.

"Yes, with the lovely brunette. Cath told me he would never come to her parties—only for a quiet dinner."

"I'm surprised that he should be caught by anything so obvious."

"As Mariella?" Tess laughed. "He'll be disappointed. She's after a husband."

"You don't think he'd . . ." Martin broke off, stunned.

"I certainly do—if he had the chance. He's not mixing with a bunch of inelegant *skaaps* because he likes them."

"I've never considered Paterson that way," said Martin slowly.

"He's lived too long in the tropics to regard women in any other light," she said.

Before Martin could reply a cascade of laughter sounded, close to them in the garden.

Mariella demanded, high-pitched: "Is that a promise, Dave? Will you take me?"

"Freetown's a long way," said Dave's sardonic tones.

"Tropical heat is unflattering to a woman's complexion and death to the finer emotions. After the first week I always thrash my women black and blue."

"Really?"

Below his breath, Martin murmured, "She believes him."

And equally low, Tess answered, "So do I."

The next moment the couple appeared, sauntering on the path, Dave tall and broad in a light suit, his hands thrust carelessly into his trousers pockets, and Mariella all pink and cream and bobbing black tresses.

Dave had raised his head towards the two on the veranda, and paused. "That can't be you, Teresa."

"That could be you, Mr. Paterson," she returned with the same inflexion. "Good evening, Mariella."

Dave said coolly: "Mind if I break it up? I'd like a word with you, Tess."

Mariella had drifted to Martin's side.

"Shall we go indoors?" he said politely.

Tess remained leaning against a veranda post. The light from the room behind silhouetted her head and shoulders, throwing into relief the cap of pale curls and gleaming over their surface.

Dave's lifted brow shone like copper: his smile was very white. "Come down here. I'll help you."

In slacks she would have been over in a second, disdaining assistance. Now, she turned and used the steps. When she reached him he put his head on one side, surveying her from the topmost curl to her waist.

For half a minute her stare challenged him. Then: "What am I supposed to do? Smack your face?"

"Were my thoughts so blatant?" He grinned, and added accusingly, "I believe you're letting your hair grow, too."

"Aren't you wasting your technique? I'm not Mariella."

They had begun to walk along the path between aloes and Canary palms.

"Wholesome little piece, isn't she?" he said conversationally. "She hasn't quite your intelligence, Teresa, but she's instinctively wise about handling men."

"I'm sure of that." High-voiced, she mimicked,

"Do you really thrash your women, Dave?"

He nipped the arm that swung beside him. "I'd certainly get some relief out of chastising you, my child. You're my biggest headache."

"Which I take to mean that you haven't yet cabled my father," she said, carefully excluding all antagonism from her voice. "I'm very grateful."

"I came tonight purposely to see you about it," he curtly told her.

"I live just down the lane," she softly reminded him.

"It occurred to me that on neutral ground we stood more chance of observing the conventions." Tess had no time to analyse this before he ended, "Has your father fixed on a date for his return?"

"He's sailing from Rio in about five weeks and I believe the trip takes nearly a month." She cast a sideways glance at him. "Will you leave it over that long?"

"It depends on Cramer."

For Martin's sake she lied. "You misjudge him. Martin's not a man in love."

"The signs are pretty obvious. I'm not blind. Something is holding him back, but with a man of his type there always comes a snapping point. I mean him to be gone before that happens."

She slowed and he, perforce, did the same, and faced her. The night breeze quivered through her dress and seemed to affect her voice.

"Martin's going through a period of strain. We can't complicate his life at this juncture." Briefly, she explained about the forthcoming examination by a specialist in Johannesburg. "So you see, we've got to keep him happy and optimistic. About his . . . emotions, where I'm concerned," she avoided the unswerving gaze, "I'm convinced it's a mental symptom of his physical condition. He's becoming more fit every day, and, well—"

"He's wanting a woman," Dave brutally supplied. "Isn't that what I've been trying to ram into you?"

"It isn't as crude as that," she cried. "Two years ago he had to renounce all idea of a normal life, and now . . ." She threw out a hand. "You're a man — can't you guess how he must feel?"

"I can," he said, grimly mocking. "I am also aware that where your affections lie you can be an absolute fool. However, from what I've seen of Cramer, he's inherently decent. He'd need encouragement to go the whole way with you."

A silence stretched between them. Dave offered cigarettes and, when she refused, lit one for himself. Tess saw the perpetually glowing tip close to his mouth but forbore to ask whether he always smoked so furiously; tonight he seemed bent on devastatingly plain speaking.

"If I were you," she advised, "I'd go in and prise Mariella from her present partner. She'll make you forget this session with me."

"Quite," he agreed with acidity. "Making love used to be the antidote for most ills in the tropics. We'd have considered ourselves blessed by all the gods if there had been anything on hand as delicious as Mariella."

She shrugged. "You're among plenty of women now. Why the grudge?"

There was a harshness in his reply. "I've been looking forward to settling in a place like Zinto for a long time — too long. Now I've got it, it tastes flat."

"After only four months?"

"I did a stupid thing — I didn't cut clean from the tropics. There's a tin mine at Lokola in which I still own a half-share."

"Oh." Her curiosity and interest had warmed. "Where's Lokola?"

"On the West Coast, about a hundred miles inland."

"Couldn't you sell out now?"

"Probably."

"You'd rather keep it, though." Thoughtfully, she had a peach to her teeth, tearing off the skin. "I wonder what made you retain a link with West Africa? After all . . ."

Forcibly, he grasped the peach and flung it away. "Your passion for fruit-stealing will land you in prison, or in hospital," he snapped irritably. "That

39

peach has been hanging in the dust for months."

From which little outburst Tess gathered that he regretted her brief invasion of his privacy, and that she had better forget what she had just learned about him.

By now they were back on the path below the veranda. The gramophone still crooned and young folk still danced and laughed, but Mariella sat on the steps alone, her pink skirt wide, her skin freshly powdered. She looked cool, but sounded breathless.

"You've missed three dances. What on earth did you find to talk about?"

Dave bowed. "Chiefly you, Mariella, and some business besides."

"What about the drive you promised me?"

"Did I?" He smiled urbanely. "Will you pardon us, Teresa? We have a date with the moon."

Benignly, Tess inclined her head. "I hope you'll *both* have fun. Good night, Mariella. Good night, Mr. Paterson."

She entered Cath's lounge, vexed to realize that she was listening exclusively to the receding purr of Dave's sedan.

After that evening, Tess kept clear of Inchfaun. An unseasonable storm provided the first excuse and it was not difficult to fabricate others as occasion necessitated.

She was not altogether cut off from Mariella Carr. That good-looking young woman had taken to borrowing Everard Arnold's tourer and driving down most mornings for a dip in Dave's pool. She must have bathed alone, for Dave was increasingly occupied with the citrus harvest and new planting, but as the clock was invariably moving towards one when she rounded the bend for Inchfaun, it was reasonable to suppose that his morning's work finished in time for him to give her a drink and wave her off.

One morning Mariella pulled up and came into the store. She wore white, which startlingly enhanced her milky, thick-textured complexion. Tess, in her old blue jeans and a patched shirt, dark with sweat at each temple and grubby from handling skins, felt a tramp. But she greeted the other girl breezily.

"Lucky you, being on holiday. Wish I had time for a swim each morning."

Carefully preserving the foot of space between her dress and the counter, Mariella twisted about with an inward excitement.

"I came in for some cigarettes. Do you keep Viceroy?"

"A few. Fifty?"

"Thanks. I haven't brought any money. Will you charge them to Cath?"

"I'd rather not. You can pay next time you're this way."

Mariella tapped a varnished nail on the flat red packet and the toe of her snake-skin sandal kept pace with it. Her tongue moistened the pink-tan lips, and then, quite suddenly, she said: "Cheerio. Come up some time, won't you?" and hurried out.

Martin, who had been sitting behind the opposite counter pencilling an order, looked up with a quizzical smile. "She's in a state of exquisite torture. She'd have unloaded if I hadn't been here."

"Thank the lord you were," said Tess fervently. "Mariella's confidences might be somewhat embarrassing."

"How old is she?"

"About twenty-five."

"Time she married. She's losing her poise and becoming over-sexed."

Idly, Tess questioned, "Isn't that how men like them?"

"I don't," he answered briefly, and bent once more over the pad.

Mariella never did pay for the cigarettes. For a few more mornings she went up to the farm and then her visits abruptly ended. Tess concluded that Dave was working at the other end of the estate, and that for Mariella the pool alone was insufficient attraction.

Tess had forgotten Mariella till the morning when little Hazel Arnold, Cath's offspring, tripped into the store and loudly proclaimed to Jacob that she sought his "missus." Tess came out from the office.

"Goodness, Hazel," she exclaimed, to the child's delight, "don't tell me you came all that way on your new pony!"

"Course not" — though she swaggered — "my mommie's outside in our car. She says you're to go out and speak to her, but I have to stay with Martin and not make myself a nuisance."

"Martin's busy. Jacob will look after you and give you some lollipops."

Cath Arnold sat behind the wheel, her panama pushed back to reveal an anxious frown. "Morning, Tess. Come and sit with me."

"Trouble?" Tess slid into the seat and pulled shut the door. "Everard's not ill?"

"No. In some ways it's worse than that." Seen close, Cath's plain face had a look almost of disaster. "I'm awfully worried about Mariella."

"Is she still with you?"

"This is her last week. I've been puzzling for days what could be wrong with her and last night she told me. She's in love with Dave Paterson — not just infatuated — but desperately, heartbreakingly in love."

It took Tess some seconds to absorb this. Before she could comment Cath spoke again.

"Dave flattered her at the beginning and she fell headlong. She's town-bred, and Dave's worldliness captured her. I dare say you've seen her on her way up to Zinto for a swim?"

"Not lately."

Cath sighed. "No, not lately. Apparently he put over some story about working too far from home to get back to lunch, so she gave that up. He hasn't been over to see us recently, so yesterday I sent him an invitation to supper. I expressly mentioned that this was Mariella's last week, but he declined. She read his note and it all came out."

"Poor Mariella. Couldn't she see that he's not the marrying kind? You should have warned her, Cath."

"I hardly knew it myself," she replied unhappily. "He's settled here, and what more natural than his taking a wife? At one time I even hoped it might be

Mariella. She's normally placid and would suit a man of his temperament."

"It can't be so very serious. She hasn't known him long enough." Recalling Dave's remarks the night she had met him at Inchfaun, Tess asked, "Has he made love to her?"

"Lightly, I believe. He's so practised, and she was willingly deceived."

So Mariella's "instinctive wisdom in handling men" had been lavished without result upon Dave Paterson. Tess was not surprised. He had probably realized quite early in the friendship that for all her naked shoulders and archness the girl was basically innocent, and lost interest in the pursuit.

"I came to you," Cath was saying, "because Mariella begged me to. She has a notion that if you were to ask Dave down to your house for dinner and invite her, too — with Martin as a fourth — she would have a chance of being alone with him. I told her it was rather hopeless."

Soberly, Tess observed: "She must be sunk, to grovel like that. Dave's never been inside my house. He'd think I'd gone mad."

"But you could try it, Tess."

Tess said queerly, "*You* don't expect me to do it?"

"Is it pleading for so very much? Put yourself in Mariella's place — or thank God from the bottom of your heart that you're not in it. Love with no outlet is a terrible thing."

"He'll say no, and Mariella will drown a second time."

"But we must attempt it for her, Tess."

After Cath and the sticky Hazel had departed, Tess wondered if she had given in too easily. She hated the thought of Dave entering her lack-lustre rooms, being sarcastic to Martin, inflicting the death-blow on Mariella, and driving carelessly home with a tune on his lips.

With foreboding, at twelve-thirty, she drove out the jeep. The track was smoother than when she had last come this way, and the pickers were industriously stripping the Valencias, canvas bags slung over their shoulders and bright, oiled clippers in hand.

Tess stopped the jeep under the green spikes of a palm. Her knees actually trembled, but she sternly commanded herself to remember Mariella, and use control. Nevertheless, she could not hurry to the dazzling, open lawn.

A boy, whose confiding smile she connected with Dave's grocery lists, came out to tell her that the boss was not yet here. Would she please sit down and drink? She recognized the formula and firmly stated that she preferred to wait in the garden. By the time Dave, apprised of her presence by his boy, had joined her, her resolution was wilting.

"Hello," she said awkwardly.

"Hello to you. What's biting?"

He was grimy, his shirt clung with sweat and he was tired with a morning in the sun. She wished profoundly that she had not come.

"It's a friendly call, though I dare say I could have chosen a better hour for it. Will you come down and have dinner with me tomorrow night?"

His eyes narrowed. "Why — expecting a police raid?"

"You needn't be insulting."

"I'm afraid I distrust you in hospitable mood. Tell me outright what's wrong and I'll do what I can to help."

"Nothing's wrong. I'm merely asking you to dinner."

"Not without a motive — not you. Let's reverse it, and you come here."

"Alone?"

An unpleasant little smile pulled back one corner of his mouth. "I see. You're planning a party. Count me out, little one."

Tess drew a rueful breath. "I suppose there is a way of approaching you that gets results. You're not completely insensitive."

"That line won't get you anywhere, either. Mariella bores me, more so since she has you enlisted as Cupid."

Tess was stung by his half-sneering tone. "You made love to her, raised her to some seventh heaven and left her to slide out of it as best she could. You're

44

enjoying a silent laugh at her expense . . ."

"Now, now, no histrionics!"

"You're a brute and a beast. It wouldn't tax you to meet her for the last time and be pleasant. You owe her that."

"My dear child, if anything, Mariella owes me a bit. I suffered her for weeks before showing her the door, and it's hardly my fault if she fancies herself in love with me."

"So you don't care?"

"I don't intend losing sleep over it, and you're an idiot to become involved in the business."

"Well, that seems to dispose of the matter."

She began retracing her way to the jeep, with Dave close behind. He caught at her elbow. "Come in and have lunch with me."

"No, thanks. Katie has mine ready. Besides, I'd rather not look at you for a few days."

His laugh was grim. "We judge these affairs from opposing viewpoints. The fact of being loved by someone entails no obligation. Perhaps it's unholy in me to compare Mariella with Cramer — he's of finer stuff, and your relationship with him is purely intellectual . . . isn't it?"

A faint bitterness crept into her voice. "I'm not in love with Martin, but I could never hurt him as you've hurt Mariella. If I did, it would stay with me for the rest of my life."

She did not linger to experience more of his cynicism. Everything he said seemed to have sharp edges, and they were beginning to stab her bewilderingly, so that she was afraid his next remark would turn in her heart, like a sword.

Her foot on the accelerator, she sat looking before her at the speeding track, stubbornly ignoring her emotions as one might strive to ignore a leopard in the undergrowth, hoping it would vanish before one looked again. She had to brake and draw in under the pines which flanked her gate, to sit with arms crossed on the wheel, her fingers clinging to it as one clings to ease a physical pain, her head down, her mind fighting an unconquerable tide.

Half an hour passed before she could stir to go

indoors and put into words on notepaper Dave s refusal to bid farewell to Mariella.

CHAPTER FOUR

MARTIN was preparing for his trip to Johannesburg. They had decided to leave his rickety sports car in the garage. Tess would drive him to Greenside, which was on the main line, and from there he would catch an express from the coast. Owing to the infrequency of the train service he would be gone six days. He complained that six days was much too long.

During the last month his features had sharpened, heightening his aesthetic good looks. It was natural that he should be anxious, but Tess, examining him at odd moments, thought his worries groundless. She prayed that the doctor would give him the news he craved; prayed it as much for herself as for him, for if Martin were free and whole her immediate problem would be resolved. Quite soon, her father would be back and they could discuss the future. Never before had the future assumed such importance.

She and Martin went to Parsburg to buy his ticket and a new suitcase. They had dinner at the hotel and looked in at the tiny town hall for an hour to watch a very old film. When they came out into the cool, starry night he tucked her arm in his and set out briskly for the car park. She returned his smile.

"You forgot the haircut, Martin."

"So I did. Does it look awful?"

"Longish at the back, but it suits you."

"I'll try to remember to have it off as soon as I reach Jo'burg." He squeezed her arm against his side. "We must do this often when I come back. If all goes well I'll trade in the old bus for a new one. There ought to be another cheque in the mail soon."

"Then when Ned's here — if he's all right — we could go to the coast for a short holiday. I haven't been to the sea for nearly three years."

"Haven't you?" He looked at her tenderly. "You've had a strange sort of life for a girl, haven't you?

46

I'd like to give you all the things you've missed."

"Incidentally," she said quietly, "they'd coincide with things you've missed, too. You don't have to walk so fast for me, Martin."

"Sorry. Tonight I feel like running and singing."

He did hum to himself in the car, and even cruised along for a while with his left arm across her back. At the house he got out with her and held wide the gate. It closed between them, but they remained near, holding hands in a familiar, amicable way. Then he let her fingers go and took light hold of her shoulders, pressing her to him while his face hid in her hair.

"You're not putting up with this to be kind?" he whispered unsteadily.

"Don't be silly."

"I can feel your heart beating."

"Yours is doing overtime."

"Tess," his clasp tightened, "you're so wonderfully sweet. I'm scared of losing you."

"You're being silly again."

"Damned silly," he agreed, and a tremor ran through him.

She felt the movement of his mouth close to her ear, the shy exploration of his hands over her shoulder-blades and the gate denting the soft flesh of her side. After which there was coldness where his warmth had been.

"Good night," he muttered, and swiftly got into the car.

The following Friday they left early for Greenside. In a new grey suit with a darker grey silk shirt and a crocus-blue tie, Martin looked young and handsome. While they wound over dun-coloured hills and through somnolent dorps, he enlarged upon a couple of ideas which he hoped to expand into articles on his way north.

"It's funny," he said. "When I first came to Zinto I could only write in the quietest surroundings, and here I'm planning to utilize a train journey. Your influence again, Tess."

"Good food and plenty of sleep," she corrected him. "I hope you'll find a quiet hotel."

47

"It won't matter. One of these days I'll take you to Johannesburg just to show you how lucky you are not to live there."

The train came in a quarter of an hour late and remained at the platform for twenty minutes. Both Tess and Martin chafed at those twenty minutes for whatever they said was a repetition of earlier conversation and neither relished an atmosphere of anticlimax. Tess boarded the train and inspected Martin's bunk, stood with him in the corridor and watched the native children playing in the rubble street of a small location of railway workers. The sordidness was appalling.

With a sense of release she heard the slam of carriage doors and hurried from the carriage with Martin. The world was right side up again, bustling and vivid. He held both her wrists.

"There won't be time for corresponding, Tess."

"No. I'll meet the train next Wednesday."

"Good-bye, my dear."

"Good-bye." Involuntarily, she raised her lips, and was conscious of his rush of gratitude and devotion as he kissed them. "Good luck, Martin. Good-bye."

He sprawled from the window, long hair whipped forward by the gathering speed of the train, which gradually vanished into the midday haze. Beset by a sudden loneliness, Tess hastened to the jeep and set it moving.

It was in a depressed frame of mind that she went home to supper and to a lesser degree the melancholy mood persisted throughout the week-end. In the days before Martin, when Zinto had stood empty and her only companions were natives, she had never been lost for tasks to fill her leisure. But at the moment, even the old guitar failed her; she must have grown out of its adolescent appeal.

When Dave was working near home he used a gelding instead of the car. The rhythm of a horse under him reminded him of polo at Lokola and the races on the West Coast. It set him thinking about Brigham, Redding and Walton, who had derided his ambition to settle on a farm. They had even offered five to one on his crawling back to Lokola within a year. They would have lost; it was already sixteen months since he had sailed from Accra.

Brigham had written that the mine looked like paying at last. If he wished to sell out there would be no more profitable time than the present. Dave's reply had told him to mind his own business; no tippling tin-miner was going to advise him about his investments. It did him good to see his own flow of profanity staring up from the notepaper.

Since the peak of the season had passed he had taken to returning mid-morning to the veranda for a refresher. Today, he reined in at the Marais bungalow on his way up, and called to Piet, who was drinking his mug of coffee in the yard with a youngster tugging at each trouser leg.

"Did you send for that seed, Marais?"

"The boy just got back." Apologetically, Piet shook off his encumbrances and came across to the low fence. "They made him take the lot in a packing-case — said sacks are still scarce."

"He could have borrowed a dozen at the store on his way up."

"I asked him why he didn't and he said the store's closed."

Dave pondered. "That's odd. Didn't he see anyone?"

"Only old August Mkize. Seems that Tess opened at eight and shut up shop an hour later."

"She's well?"

"I guess so — she always is. But I'll send down again, if you like."

"No," said Dave, "I'm going that way myself."

He backed out the car and nosed it down the track at more than his usual speed. This was Monday and Cramer was not due back till Wednesday. Maybe he should have followed his inclinations yesterday and come down to see her; she couldn't still be upset over that Carr girl. Though Tess Bentley's reactions to anything were incalculable.

The Bentley house looked about as drab and lifeless as ever. He drove round, parked at the corner and

49

remained in his seat, speculating. The store was shuttered, not merely locked up for an hour or two while she went into Parsburg. And then he noticed the swaying door of the garage and the jeep inside. Tess must be in the house—in the house, and the store shuttered. What the hell?

He was out of the car and striding across the yard, through the thin line of gum trees and into the wilderness of a garden. At the foot of the steps he had to pause, for Tess was coming out and closing the door behind her. In her white shirt and a short, red skirt made from one of her old dresses she looked about fifteen, but her face had tragic lines of maturity. The blue eyes flickered at him, she took a firmer grasp of her bag and descended to the path.

"What is it?" he said quietly.

Her head bent and he saw her eyes close and her jaw go taut. Her voice had the roughness of swallowed pain.

"I had an air letter this morning from a man in Rio. My father's dead."

Instinctively, his arm went round her. "Oh, God. Tell me about it."

She couldn't, for a minute. Her shoulder leaned into his chest and she shivered with a fresh surge of grief.

"He said that Ned collapsed with a heart attack and died almost at once. It happened a fortnight ago, a couple of days before he was supposed to sail."

There was nothing Dave could say to lessen her hurt. He raked through her hair, pushing her head hard against his collar-bone, and felt a hot tear soak through his shirt to his skin.

"Where were you going?" he asked presently.

She tried to straighten. "I've just written to my brothers, but hadn't any airmail stamps. I could have sent Jacob, but I thought the trip into Parsburg would give me something to do."

"Quite right," he agreed. "I'll take you."

As he freed her she turned away. "Sorry to have collapsed upon you like that. I'd have done the same with any white man who'd turned up just then."

"That's all right," he said. "I won't take advantage of it. Let's get moving."

They were some miles along the road when she

thanked him. "I'll have to do whatever you say about the store," she added.

"Will your brothers be coming?"

"They can't, very well. Gerald is on the verge of exams and Alan can't afford the time away from his studies, either. I've told them in the letters that there's nothing they can do."

"Neither, of course, would admit responsibility for a younger sister."

"They know I'm perfectly able to take care of myself."

"They'll also realize, in time, that you're no longer running the store for their benefit."

"Gerald will be passing into a hospital, but it will come hard on Alan. He's the younger—only twenty-three."

"Is that all?" with satire. "Poor Gerald may have to dig into his savings for his little brother. Was there a will?"

"Yes, it's with the lawyer. We're each to have a third."

Dave was on the point of saying, "So your father did possess that much humanity," but he changed it to: "Oh, well, they'll have a few hundred each, anyway. The stock should fetch a bit."

Tess didn't enquire what he had in mind. Being with Dave drew her from under the pall of sadness but, as yet, kindled no fires. When he swept past the store and up the lane, she put no questions, though as he helped her from the car outside his own house, she did demur in low tones.

"I can't keep wasting your time like this."

He smiled. "Am I being too kind? Makes you wish you'd treated me better, doesn't it? Never mind. From now on, you can atone."

"What about your work?"

"To hell with it. Any good on a horse?"

"I used to be — as a kid, but I can't ride now."

"Yes, you can. My chestnut will fit you. Come on, we'll try her out."

When he said good night to her late on the veranda of her house, he smiled down into her small, colourless face.

"You won't start pitying yourself as soon as you're alone, will you? These losses happen to everyone."

She blinked treacherous moisture from her eyes. "You're so different that I'm not sure what to say to you."

"Not yet," he said, "but the time will come."

Her expression was startled. "You mean . . ."

"I mean," he explained evenly, "that next time you start spitting at me I shall know exactly how to act. Now go to bed and sleep. I'll come down in the morning."

He came after breakfast next morning, let that critical gaze of his rove over her face and gave her chin a friendly tap. He decreed that the store remain closed till Thursday, when Martin could take over. Apparently he had plans for today; another ride—so she had better wear slacks; a swim, and this afternoon a canoe up the river.

Tess made no attempt to analyse his generosity. She acquiesced in everything he suggested and was even faintly pleased when he complimented her swimming.

When the sun had gone they sat on the veranda and listened to the crickets chirring their love-songs and the palms gossiping over the day's happenings.

Dave cut short a tranquil silence. "What time is Cramer supposed to get in tomorrow?"

"At Greenside? Around four. I shall leave at two-thirty to meet him."

"You're not going to meet him."

"No?" There had been a note in his lazy voice which made her careful. "I promised."

"That was last Friday. Your boy can take Cramer's car to the junction and he can drive himself."

Slowly she said: "I couldn't do that to Martin. He'll want to talk."

"Well, he must wait. That young man is too full of himself. Some time soon he'll have to leave Zinto and he may as well become accustomed to small hardships right away. You're spoiling him for an independent life."

"I don't agree." She spoke reasonably, from freshly acquired knowledge of how to deal with him. "During his six months here he's gained poise and confidence."

"And your sympathy. Before long, sympathy won't be enough."

"You haven't cited a single reason why I shouldn't keep my promise tomorrow. I'd hate to anger you over this, but I would feel wretched if I broke it."

His answer was so long in coming that Tess wondered if already, in this new peace between them, a rift was starting. Then he swung one bare knee over the other, flipped open his silver case and selected a couple of cigarettes.

"Heaven forbid that I should enter into a tug-of-war with you over the store assistant," he said. "Shall I light your cigarette or would you prefer to do it yourself?"

"You light it."

He struck a match and illuminated an enigmatic grin on the well-cut lips. They smoked in quietude till the boy, Ephraim, began to clatter the cutlery for dinner.

"I've been thinking about the store," he said, his manner altered. "We'll put up the whole thing for sale—buildings and land. There's no petrol pump or bottle store attached, but the turnover is plenty for a man with a small family. What is the stock worth?"

"It's low at the moment. Between a thousand and fifteen hundred."

"And say another two thousand for the goodwill. I suppose the house should stand up for another ten years—we'll ask six thousand, and take five. You and your brothers should net about seventeen hundred each."

"Only the stock and goodwill are ours."

"The land is worth nothing to me and I refuse to own such buildings. You'd like your brothers to do well out of the sale, wouldn't you?"

"Not at your expense," she said flatly. "You despise them."

"If it weren't for feeling that you deserve so much better from them I might appreciate their position. Let's not argue about money, Tess. In the long run it means very little."

True enough. She had lived happily without it. But it looked as if Dave were putting her dangerously in his debt.

"I'll place the proposition with a couple of estate agents," he said. "The sale will take time—perhaps three months. Marais may know someone who'll take over temporarily, and I'll mention a tempting salary as bait."

Half of her gave in; it was so sweet to be bossed. The other half was fearful. How would she exist with nothing to do? And what of Martin? Was she, when the numbness of grief had faded, going to be able to bear Dave's domination?

She quivered and withdrew her arm.

"Going off cold?" he queried. "Come in and have some whisky."

Quickly, she got up and preceded him indoors. "I can't take it like your tropical women. One whisky makes a soak out of me."

"Never been tight?"

"No. Ought I?"

He shrugged, his eyes glinting at some private thought. "There's a lot to be said for trying everything once. We'll resume this discussion at a later date, my sweet. Tonight you'll take a nip in a glass of very plain water."

To Martin, at least, Ned Bentley's death brought a temporary relief. The long journey down from Johannesburg had been grilling in every sense of the word, and the salutary shock of meeting a Tess gone quiet and desolate was what he needed in order to view his own unhappiness in its true proportions. After all, he was very much alive and had twice the energy of a year ago. The specialist had stated that he had as much chance of living well into the mellow years as anyone else . . . if he took care.

A little desperately, Martin had told the man that he wanted to get married. The sandy eyes had contracted behind the strong lenses, and the loose, elderly mouth had squared.

"I'm going to be frank with you, my boy. You're doing fine, and you seem to have chosen a spot which suits you, physically and temperamentally. My advice is that you continue whatever you are doing now and forget about complications. I'm not forbidding you to have a woman now and then, but marriage at this stage of your cure is out of the question."

Wretchedly, Martin had muttered, "She's very understanding."

"My dear chap," the doctor had sternly asserted, "no healthy girl could stand wholesale frustration for the first two years of her marriage, and I doubt if you'd be strongwilled enough to impose it. It would be disastrous for both of you. If she cares enough, she'll wait."

So, when he had absorbed the news Tess had given him and she asked for his, Martin merely answered, "The old boy was pleased with my condition—said I'll live to be a hundred if I don't overdo things."

"That's good. I knew you were better."

"It looks as if I shall have to take up permanent quarters in the Zinto district."

Tess was unable to offer the reassurance he desired. She kept silent, hardly aware that by doing so she gave her consent, should circumstances permit. She was too familiar with his character to believe that he had told her the whole, for where she was concerned Martin could not dissimulate.

He settled back into the store as if he had never been away, but as it became patent that Tess now confined her activities to office work he was strained and uneasy. After a few days he taxed her with it.

"Dave Paterson demanded it," she told him simply. "While my father leased the store I could defy him, but for the present we have to do whatever he dictates." She tried to prepare him, "Dave hates the store; he may try to cut it off from his property."

"Would he consider us as tenants and potential buyers?" Painful colour crept up from his throat. "We might even buy at once, and apply for a mortgage bond. My writing would take care of repayments."

"It's sweet of you, Martin, but he seems to have other ideas. If controlling the shop on your own is too much for you——"

"Of course it isn't. The boys do the donkey work."

"Well, we must hope that he'll do nothing in a hurry. I'm no more anxious to leave Zinto than you are."

This pleased Martin. He smiled at her gratefully, and the two lines which had etched themselves between his brows faded a little.

Emerging from her loss, Tess began to notice in him a fatalistic acceptance of his own limitations, though there were still moments when he grew hollow-eyed and pale with the intensity of his thoughts; moments when she was afraid to speak lest those thoughts be revealed. With returning zest came also a repugnance towards intimate discussion with Martin. She was no less fond of him, but a deeper, more desperate emotion was beginning to swathe her head and her heart.

Every couple of days Dave called to see her, timing his visit to coincide with morning coffee or afternoon tea. They talked of crops and cattle and neighbours, and she avoided the subject of Martin until the day when he told her that as Cramer seemed to be handling things satisfactorily he might as well stay in the job till the place was sold, and take a salary as manager. Tess was too thankful to probe the object behind the decision. She merely thanked him and made a light reference to the fact that between the store and his writing, Martin was putting in too many hours to have time for much else.

Since those two evenings just after the news of Ned's death, Tess had not been to the farmhouse for dinner. She had played tennis there in the early evening and stayed for a sundowner, but each time she was driven home at seven. Then one day, about a month after Martin's return, Dave invited her to dinner the following evening.

With faint emphasis he ended, "You haven't made other arrangements?"

"You know I never go out!"

"Tomorrow is different, surely."

"Oh!" Her blankness gave way to a half-smile. "Who told you it's my birthday?"

"Mrs. Marais, a long time ago. Like lots of things about you, it registered in my memory, never to be forgotten." His grin teased. "Twenty's a great age, a whole decade removed from nineteen."

"I shall only be a day older."

56

"And a day nearer heaven," he said mockingly. "It's time you fell in love."

She bent over the pouring of second cups of tea, and casually enquired, "How would you like to be my first affair?"

He laughed, and deliberately plopped a knob of sugar into the milk jug. "I should imagine an affair with you might be brief, tempestuous and somewhat shattering, but we'd both learn plenty. A year after it finished we'd still be getting our wind."

"Sounds exciting," she said regretfully, and slid his cup across the veranda table, "though it might spoil one for a normal existence. Perhaps I ought to start with someone less experienced and work up to the expert."

He leaned back on two legs of his chair, his glance a pleasant taunt. "I rather think, Teresa, that nothing but the best will satisfy you. Let me know when your heart becomes unruly."

She stirred her tea. "Will there be other guests tomorrow?"

"I'll send a note to the Arnolds, if you like."

"I'd rather not make a public occasion of it."

"So would I," he remarked non-committally, and ten minutes later he left her.

Martin, too, knew that next day was her birthday. He arrived early and gave her an enamel and ormolu powder compact which he had bought in Johannesburg for this purpose. He kissed her cheek and voiced the hope that he would be able to give her something more valuable and intimate next year.

Tess couldn't have explained her reluctance to encounter him, but it stayed with her all day. By six it was dark, and she dressed by lamplight in a green tailored linen dress, and combed her lengthening curls into a bunch at the back of her head. When Dave came, she hurried down the path and met him in the gateway.

"Happy birthday, Teresa," he said softly, and then, mockingly aware of her tenseness, "Had a scare?" She shook her head. "Forget it."

The short drive with Dave at her side did not dispel the strange upheaval in her veins, and her nerves still quivered when he was pouring drinks in the lounge, though by then she could smile and accept his good wishes as they sipped.

After a moment he took her glass and placed it on a low table beside his own. From his pocket he produced a small cubic case. He snapped it open and her heart gave a frightened leap. The ring was gold set with an exquisite oval of Chinese jade in a surround of small diamonds.

"Ever owned a dress-ring?" he asked offhandedly, and pushed it along the third finger of her right hand. "Looks nice."

The hand trembled. "Dave . . ."

"Well?" He was smiling. "Don't you like it?"

She pressed the ring to her flaming cheek. "I love it. I don't know how to thank you."

"It's easy," he murmured, his hands upon her shoulders, the grey eyes glittering.

But Tess wasn't yet ready for his lips. Her arms curved about his neck and her face moved against his jacket. His grip of her tightened, hurting her chest and driving the air from her lungs. He forced her to raise her head and part her mouth to his long, bruising kiss.

As he released her the boy came in to announce that dinner was ready.

"Probably been watching us through the crack of the door," Dave said, not looking at her. He drained his sherry. "How's your appetite, Teresa?"

"Hardly improved by . . . that," she managed. "You might have warned me."

"Surely you expected a birthday kiss?"

Under her breath she said, "Is that what it was?" and she passed him to enter the dining-room.

She was glad when Dave suggested taking coffee on the veranda. Though the night was by no means cold, the air had sufficient freshness to clear her brain.

When he poured whisky she declined. "No more drink. I'm hot enough." She sniffed. "Smells faintly acrid, like a storm."

He came beside her. "Supposing one started now — what would you do?"

"Let you take me home before the track flooded."

"And if I refused?"

Tess smiled round at him. "I'd have to run all the way." She turned back again. "Your orange trees are budding. I can smell them."

"In a week or two they'll be overpowering and I shall be sorry I chose to farm citrus."

There was a silence. Then, swiftly, she twisted and moved a pace or two away from him.

"I'd better go home, Dave."

"It's only ten."

"Still — I ought to go."

"Wouldn't you rather have a swim?"

Startled, she met the provoking glint in his glance. Her own wide eyes were full of the lamplight and her skin glowed. "A swim? I've never bathed at night. But I haven't a swimsuit."

"You left yours here this morning. I found it when I took a dip before lunch and hung the pieces on a bush. The boy will have put it in the kitchen."

"I'll find it."

"Go into the kitchen and change," he called after her. "I'll bring you a robe."

The kitchen was as spruce as only a well-trained native could make it, and her swim-suit, neatly ironed and folded, lay ostentatiously on the seat of a white-enamelled chair. Tess dragged on the briefs and performed the usual contortion to tie the strings of the brassière. Odd, the indecency of bathing wear within walls. Dave ought to have brought the robe along at once and dropped it outside the door.

He knocked. "Ready?"

She opened the door and he held out a burgundy silk dressing-gown.

"You'd better have this — it's shorter than the bathrobe. There's nothing to blush about, Teresa. You once lay in my bed like that."

"I hope you had nightmares afterwards."

"I did," he admitted succinctly, tightening the girdle of the bath-robe round his middle. "Hold up your skirt or you'll trip on your nose."

An extraordinary sensation seized her. She raced out of the house before him, tearing like a mad thing

59

down the garden path. He loped behind, not attempting to catch her up till laughter floated over her shoulder. Sweet, elusive laughter. He spurted and grabbed the flying dressing-gown, but she was out of it, fleeing ahead like a wind-borne goddess. As he shook off his robe she cleaved the water, and he waited till the pale head came up ten feet away before flinging himself upon her.

That struggle with Dave in the moon-shot pool had a savage, pagan quality. At times Tess could see his teeth, set in a devilish grin. However she kicked she could not evade the crushing strength of his arms, and when at last she was spent except for the leaping, molten thing that was her heart, he had her helpless and kissed her mouth.

"I'll teach you to dare me," he grunted, and kissed her again, so thoroughly that his legs ceased to move and they both sank under.

Tess surfaced free of him. She tossed back her hair and made for the stone steps, grasped one of them and paused to regain her balance. Suddenly, the ominous silence of the pool smote her. She peered over the water and saw it black, with dancing silver hills.

"Dave!" she cried sharply. The sound echoed in her ears, but she shouted again, more peremptorily.

Stop shaking, she sternly bade herself. Men like Dave didn't drown in a dozen feet of water. He must be lurking at the far end, laughing at her. No one could stay submerged for so long.

She strove to keep her tone level. "Dave, I've had enough. I'm getting out."

Still that oppressive noiselessness. Fighting down the panic that rasped in her throat, she pushed back into the water and struck out for the opposite end; she even swam under water for a while, but at length had to gasp her way to the side and pull herself clear. She slumped on the grass, her head down upon her knees, her whole body vibrating with the effort to breathe.

Hard, dry hands grasped her upper arms. She stiffened, and raised her head to look into a face gone angular with some sort of emotion. His shoulders gleamed like polished stone but the one that slipped behind her was warm and vital.

"Tess, I'm terribly sorry. I didn't think for a second you'd take it seriously. I ducked behind the rubber plants."

"Swine," she choked, and cracked a bony little fist at his chin.

And then the fight went out of her. She lay in his arms, wanting she knew not what, till his mouth descended fiercely upon hers, and found the hollow in her throat, and moved down to burn into softer flesh. Then her doubts resolved into an undeniable, flaring need.

Dave said it, a trifle thickly, for both of them: "Tess . . . Let's go indoors."

CHAPTER FIVE

DURING the following week Tess had three visits from potential buyers. Two of them were appalled by the store's isolation and the fact that the population of Parsburg was no more than three hundred whites; they were sure their wives would never settle in such a spot. The third was a bachelor of forty, engaged to a widow who would arrive in the Union about three months from now. Could he take an option on the property?

When Tess repeated this up at the farmhouse, Dave said: "Tell him an option is impossible, but we'll communicate with him before accepting another offer."

They were in the garden beneath a mango tree. It was nearly one o'clock, and Martin would be lunching with Tess today.

She reached overhead and tugged off a thick dark leaf.

"Dave, I know you're against this, but . . . couldn't you please be generous to Martin? He's not having an easy time of it just now, and it worries him that he may soon have to leave Zinto."

His smile held exasperation. "What would you have me do — present him with a partnership in the farm?

61

Why not treat him as a man and let him arrange his own life? At twenty-seven I was running a mining camp with one white assistant and a thousand Africans."

"You don't understand him a bit," she sighed. Useless to angle for Dave's sympathy when he had no intention of giving it. He softened. "You're a fool, Tess, but a lovely one. You know that men take advantage of your compassion, yet you go on giving it, with both hands. Some day you'll learn that it doesn't pay." He cupped the back of her head in the way he had, and kissed her. "Come indoors and let me kiss you properly."

"No," she answered, not very firmly. "Lovemaking puts me off my food, and Katie has prepared my favourite lunch. I'm going now."

He laughed. "All right, I'll come down later."

For a week they had met every day. Dave had at last walked through the Bentley house and shaken his head with distaste. She couldn't leave the decrepit furniture and moth-bitten *karosses* soon enough for him. Where she would thereafter take up her abode remained in the air . . . or in his mind.

It was all too new for much conjecture. She only knew that because of Dave her blood sang and her nerves leapt; that together they were one intense, concentrated life which nothing had the power to bruise. She desired no future beyond the eternal present, even though Martin had to dwell on the rim. Dave didn't realize how little was necessary to make Martin happy.

Just lunching here, across the table from Tess, brought a muted joy to his bearing. The thin cheeks, so lightly tanned, were made attractive by the faint red which had come into them; a tinge of lively green ousted the shadows from the hazel eyes and his mouth forgot the habit of compression. He ate well, and drank two cups of coffee.

It was too hot to sit on the veranda, so they subsided one each end of the rusty chesterfield to smoke a cigarette. Quite how they got on to the subject of his visit to Johannesburg neither could have traced, but Martin found himself describing the specialist's opaque, sandy eyes and shining, freckled face.

"There's something gnomish about elderly people with freckles," he mused. "I got the feeling that he would deny anybody anything in his power."

"Didn't you believe in him?"

"Up to a point, but he's a medical man, not a psychologist."

"You don't need a psychologist."

His voice changed a little. "Anyone who's been in a doctor's hands for a couple of years needs mental stimulus. All this fellow could suggest was . . . having a woman when I feel low."

Tess pressed out her cigarette in the ash-tray between them. "Maybe it's not such stupid advice. You never have . . . have you, Martin?"

"I'd hate it — with someone I didn't care for. In any case, my being in love with you makes it impossible." Martin made a complication of lighting a second cigarette, and inhaled, before mentioning, "I told him about you."

Slowly she answered, "That wasn't very wise of you," and at once wished she had kept quiet.

"It was in the cards that I'd love unwisely and behave unwisely about it, too," he said with bitterness. "I keep telling myself that I can stand it so long as you don't fall for someone else. That would be the end."

An icy hand closed round her heart. She saw Martin in the throes of a nerve-storm because he had learned of her love for Dave. Absurd. He'd merely used a common expression for emphasis. But she was afraid for his vulnerability, his seemingly fatal trend towards suffering.

The problem, his love for her and its possible effect on his work, renewed her longing to do something for him. If only Dave were not so pigheadedly opposed to Martin's control of the store they could all go on like this for many months. It was wrong to wreck Martin's peace, to turn him out of the only haven he had ever known.

Martin had stood up. "It was a grand lunch, Tess. And thanks for listening to me."

"Such a good lunch," she agreed, "that I'm sleepy. I'm going lazy for an hour. So long."

She lay on her back regarding the mottled ceiling through a haze of delicious intimate thoughts. Darkness crept in, stabbed by lightning. Another storm gathering. The spring rains were starting early, matching their violence with her own wild feelings. Life was exciting and lovely, because there was nothing she would not give Dave, no physical pain, had it been required of her, that she would not have borne for him.

They dismounted at a thicket of aloes and bottle-brush, and turned loose the horses.

Tess dug her hands into the pockets of her slacks and turned her contented gaze upon the modest Witberg heights.

"I haven't been here since before I went to college. My brothers and I came once on donkeys. The beastly things wandered and we had to walk home in the dark. It was frightful."

Dave smiled. "How old were you then?"

"About eleven. It was just before the boys sailed for England."

"When you were eleven," he said, "I'd left Cambridge and had over a year in the tropics. Does that make you think?"

Comfortably, she leaned against him. "About what — your past affairs? I've never deceived myself. Anyone can see you've been a bad lad, David, my love. It's etched all over you."

"Thanks."

Uncertain of his tone, she looked up at him, and swiftly added: "That was my rotten idea of a joke. You don't seriously want me to think up differences between us, do you? The way we are, there just aren't any."

"Sweetly put, Teresa. All the same, if I thought there weren't, I'd go round breaking a few necks." He nipped her ear. "Come and sit in the shade."

From the spot he chose they could see gentle green slopes and a brown rocky face supporting the lopsided pinnacle of the highest peak in the Witbergs.

Against the hot blue sky the scene had grandeur and an atmosphere wholly African. Far away, beyond the foothills they had penetrated, lay miles of open veld splodged with cattle which were scarcely visible at this distance. A soft wind rustled the low trees.

Dave leaned back on his elbow, his grey glance upon that craggy summit. "Ever had the urge to travel, Tess?"

She drew up her knees and hugged them. "Of course, off and on."

"To anywhere in particular?"

"Well, first it was Portuguese East Africa. Lourenço Marques isn't so very far, and it's exciting and continental."

"And expensive and sophisticated," he completed dryly. "I don't see you in Lourenço Marques — or not for long."

She wrinkled her nose at him. "You've been everywhere. Tell me about Lokola.

He paused, a faint surprise in his expression. "How did you know what was in my mind?"

"I didn't. It just came into mine. What's so fascinating about Lokola?"

"It's wet and hot and filthy. The whites drink too much and talk mud, and the Africans are the laziest I've ever come up against."

"Any women?"

"Two or three, wives of government officials, but there were none among my bunch except that Brigham, my partner, lived with a Malay girl."

"A Malay? How in the world did she get there?"

He made a small sound of amusement. "Teresa, you continually amaze me. You ought to be shocked, not caught up in the geography of the thing. Brig's a rake. His parents kicked him out of England twenty years ago and he's lived in all the slimy dumps between the Gold Coast and Singapore. He drinks, gambles, lusts, and between times he superintends the mine. While I was there I had charge of a government mine fifty miles away; the partnership with Brigham was merely a hobby that might pay dividends some time."

"You trust him?"

"Brig's all right. You won't dislike him."

She cast him a hurried, sideways glance. "Is he coming here?"

He threw back his head and laughed with pure enjoyment. "If you'd met Brig you'd appreciate how funny that is. Remind me to show you one of his letters."

Her smile palely reflected his humour. "Then . . . what did you mean?"

"That we're going to Lokola for a couple of months, you and I."

"Are we? When?"

"In about ten days." His voice sharpened. "What's the matter? Don't you fancy it?"

"Yes, but not so soon."

"This is the best time to go — while the citrus is growing. I went over to Inchfaun this morning and sounded Arnold. I think he'd be willing to keep an eye on the farm while I'm away, and Marais is well run in to my methods. The estate agent can deal with the sale of the store."

Tess picked at a snapped thread near the hem of her trouser-leg. "So that was the plan you've been hinting at?"

"I imagined it would appeal to you. It isn't every woman's idea of a honeymoon, but you're above the average."

Her colour drained and her clasp tightened round her ankles. "Honeymoon?"

There was a moment's silence while he adjusted his thoughts to hers.

"For the love of heaven!" he said harshly. "Had you decided I wasn't going to marry you? I'm not quite such a rat."

Her head was turned towards the mountain. "I — wasn't sure that you'd want marriage."

"Maybe I'm to blame for taking things too much for granted. Perhaps I should have told you that as you're under age, I had to get consent from the magistrate in Parsburg. I applied for the licence right away. We can be married in a week." His features hardened. "You don't appear to be very enthusiastic. Can't you bear to look at me?"

She slid down beside him. "Kiss me, Dave."

He did. "Why are you trembling?"

"Because I'm crazy."

"You're not happy about marrying me, are you? You believe I love you now, but you can't see it lasting. You certainly are crazy."

He kissed her with force, and she clung to him, giving back his kisses, but too choked with mixed emotions to speak.

Presently he said: "You'll need clothes — a lot of frocks and thin woollen vests. Dangerous to go about there without undies. You're going to sweat like you've never sweated before. Your vaccination mark is fairly new, isn't it?"

"Yes. There was a scare about eighteen months ago."

"That leaves only the jab for yellow fever. For safety, we'll both have it, though my last ought still to be active. Not apprehensive about fevers, are you?"

Oh, God, if only he'd be quiet. "Not a scrap," she told him, against his neck.

"You'll probably feel a bit whacked to begin with — headache and lassitude — but it'll pass, and you'll take precautions automatically. In any case, I'll be there to watch over you." She felt a vibration in his diaphragm as he tacked on: "I'm looking forward to the men's sick envy when I turn up with a wife. There never has been anything so sweet and fresh as you at Lokola. They'll adore you, Tess."

Her chest tight, her throat heavy, she stopped his mouth with a kiss so shaky and pleading that it roused him to passion. For the first time bewildering pain overlaid her ecstasy.

She was quiet as they rode back to Zinto through the gold-dusted hills, and for the rest of the evening Dave was gentle with her. He seemed to sense her shrinking from renewal of their earlier discussion and to place upon it his own satisfactory construction.

It was not till she was alone that the real torment began, and it lasted well into the night. The bitter irony of being wanted by Dave as a wife while she was bound, as an indispensable support, to Martin.

There must be a way out. Dave could be made to understand that the tug of loyalty towards Martin in no way detracted from her love for him. He was capable of pity and generosity.

But was he, where his own desires were at stake? What of Mariella? He would expect her to cast off Martin as he had shed the "Carr girl," mercilessly and with finality; whereas she, from compassion and affection, shied away from inflicting upon Martin the slightest injury. Was she a coward, undeserving of Dave's love? Tess did not think so. In Dave ran a vein of iron; if he were crossed even she would not be immune from his cruelty.

Tess got up next morning unrefreshed and dark-eyed, and no nearer an elucidation of the problem. Over at the store she watched the baling and loading of goat- and sheep-skins; a small consignment this time, because the rains had drawn up new grass upon which to feed the stock, and the natives were anxious to increase their herds.

The store oppressed. The conglomeration of odours and noises, usually tolerable at the distance of the office, sent her out into the air, and an impulse, backed by the fear that Dave might come down early, led her to get out the jeep and head for Parsburg. The straight red rutted road sped under her. She crossed the river, passed the private road up to Inchfaun and the gates to smaller farms. Mimosa thorn had clothed its winter grey with new green leaves, and the wattles dripped with pungent golden blossom. Here and there a wild peach flowered, product, presumably, of a chance-flung peach stone.

Tess drove unseeing. She entered the town and automatically pulled in at the post office. Not that she was expecting any mail, but what else could one do in town on a Monday morning? Half the shopkeepers had not yet bothered to open.

There were three letters: two from wholesalers with new lines to offer, and the other for Martin. A thin airmailed envelope, this last, from his agent. The knowledge that it probably contained a cheque bore her back in a more hopeful state of mind to Zinto.

She hurried into the store, calling his name. He appeared from the back and she stopped, made nerveless by his white, stricken face and staring eyes.

"Martin," she whispered, "what's happened?"

His hand groped towards her. "You . . . didn't know he was going to do it? Thank God."

"Who?" But already she was taut with the foreknowledge of disaster. She reached to touch him. "Dave? What has he done?"

"He came about half an hour ago." He paused, trying to control himself. "I'm fired, shown the gate. No explanation. Merely a month's salary and orders to clear off the Zinto estate today. Tess . . . darling . . ."

His voice broke, and somehow her hands locked round him, hurt and anger so strong within her that she could not think. But in a little while the desperate contraction of his arms about her slackened.

"I feel better now," he muttered, his lips to her hair. "It wasn't being told to go that mattered — only the terrible suspicion that you'd agreed on it together. Lately, I've noticed that you and he . . . well —"

"I'll speak to him," she cut in abruptly, "but I doubt if he'll climb down. You'd better take a room at the hotel in Parsburg, Martin, and I promise I'll come and see you tomorrow."

"Oh, my dear," came his anguished undertone, "I love you."

CHAPTER SIX

AFTER lunch Tess put on a pink-and-white-striped dress and went up to the farmhouse. She walked, because exercise in the heat of the day had the benefit of drugging the senses, and to feel too much in the coming interview with Dave might have a fatal effect upon its outcome.

He was on the veranda, lounging in a long chair and browsing over market bulletins. In a white shirt and khaki shorts, a cigarette between his lips and the remains of a glass of beer on the table, he looked so indolently at ease that she was able to harden against him.

"Hello," he said, and from the reserve in his manner she detected that he must have been half-expecting her. "You look very charming. I didn't hear the jeep."

"I walked."

"That was unwise, surely?"

He got up and pushed forward a chair, but she turned aside to sit on the veranda wall. He bent to kiss her, and made no comment when she kept her mouth averted from him, but straightened again, leaning back against a pillar to watch her.

"Very well, Tess. Let's have it. I'm inhuman, a heartless monster, and all the rest. Did he weep on your shoulder?"

After a moment she said, "What made you do it, without warning, or a word to me?"

"My nature, I guess. Where's the sense in arguing a case of that sort? He had to go."

"Like that?"

"As far as I'm concerned, yes. After yesterday I had no alternative."

This was perilous ground, but there could be no side-stepping it.

"Aren't you making Martin just a wee bit too important?"

"No," he said bluntly, "but you are. I was willing for him to continue as temporary manager so long as he remained just a hanger-on. But yesterday he came between us. You can't deny it, Tess," as she made to protest. "Privately, you had built up a delightful situation in which I was your lover and Cramer your intellectual soul-mate. The marriage idea jarred you back to reality."

"You seem to forget that you hadn't given me the smallest reason to suspect that you wished for marriage."

"We've been through that." Intolerance crisped his tones. "I thought this over deeply last night, and I could see no other way out. It was obvious, from the minute I mentioned Lokola, that to go away would upset the little world you'd constructed. You saw us

70

going on as we were for months, a tidy triangle. God knows what led you to believe I'd stand for it."

"I suppose I credited you with humanity and one or two other virtues. Martin could never threaten what exists between you and me."

"No?" How would you feel if I had some clinging vine of a woman in the background? Incredible though it may sound, I have my share of imagination, and I don't have to use much of it to know that Cramer touches you when he gets the chance, and works on your sympathies when he doesn't. Tell me something," he raised a foot to the wall and leaned towards her, "I wasn't the only one who did a lot of thinking last night, was I? You decided to ask me for time, so that the break with Cramer could be long-drawn and gentle. Am I right?"

"Whatever I say you'll twist, because there's something in you that won't allow you to see good in Martin. Please don't let's quarrel about this, Dave."

"My dear girl, for my part the matter's as good as closed. But I do mean to have your word that you'll never see that fellow again."

She pulled in her lip to moisten it; her glance did not waver from the green spread of the mango tree in the garden. Quietly she said: "If you love me, Dave, you won't demand the impossible. It may be all for the best that you've taken the first drastic step, but give him time to live down the unhappiness by stages. We all have something we can't take; even you, perhaps."

"I have — and this is it. You do mean to see him?"

She made no answer. He thrust back against the post, swinging down his foot with a small thud on the stone floor.

"If that's the way you feel about it," he flung at her, "you can have him. Marry him, but don't expect me to be merciful to either of you." He was suddenly furious. "What the hell d'you suppose I'm made of!"

"I don't know." She swallowed, hoping to strengthen her voice. "I'm beginning to realize that I've never understood you." She paused, and looked down at her hands upon the striped silk of her lap. "Since my father died you've been exceedingly generous.

You've arranged with the lawyer that the proceeds of the sale of the house, store and ground shall be paid to the Bentley account, and refused to accept rent though I've been banking the takings. You gave me the chestnut mare . . ."

"I shouldn't concoct any more, if I were you," he said, dangerously deliberate.

Her head rose. "You're the last person to evade facts. I'm trying to make you visualize how I was bound to regard our relationship, till you dropped the marriage bombshell."

"Let up, will you!"

"I know you love me," she said, as if he had not spoken, "but you've been in love before — without getting married. I'm not a complete fool, Dave. I'm as well aware as you are that marriage was no part of your plan when you gave me the jade and diamond ring . . ."

He blazed. His hand came up in a vicious smack at her cheek. She went very white, except where his mark began to print itself in red, and slowly got to her feet.

His nostrils were pinched, his lips drawn back upon closed teeth. "You'd better go before I really hurt you."

But it was he who went first, striding into the house and down the corridor. She heard the crack of a door, followed by a silence like the hush of death.

A quarter of an hour later she entered her own house. Katie had washed up and left the place clean and smelling of hard soap. In her room, Tess found her slacks and shirt over the back of a chair, as she had thrown them about an hour ago, and on the old dressing-table was Ned's black stud box, in which she kept the jade ring. She tore off the plastic lid and looked in at the ring. The lid snapped in her grasp, blood spurted on the pads of two fingers and she slid box and pieces back on to the dressing-table.

The room swayed. Her body was a shell of sick sensations, but her brain repeated the scene with Dave: his arrogance giving way to anger, and the anger to something white-hot and ungovernable.

72

It wasn't over, of course. Tonight he would come down as he always did, and she would go more than half-way to meet his apology. He'd hate himself, and she would tell him how little anything mattered beside the fact of their need for each other. They would be married next week and leave for Lokola. Martin could do what he liked — shoot himself or go native; she would promise Dave never to go near him again.

Loneliness throbbed in her like an acute ache; loneliness and heart-wrenching worry. After a while she had a bath and went to bed. Towards morning she fell into a doze, from which an astonished Katie roused her. Tess sent her away and tried to climb back over the ridge into unconsciousness, but recollection, as inexorable as the sun, flooded over her.

When she had dressed there was nothing to do. She thought of Martin as of some remote acquaintance whom she might never see again. She sat on the step, in order to glimpse the sedan the moment it appeared in the lane. Would Dave stop, or merely wave and drive on? She couldn't go on suffering like this.

By the afternoon, when it became almost certain that he would not go to town, Tess had decided to buy something to read. She drove slowly into town. But it was impossible to browse in a bookshop empty of other customers, so she chose a novel and some magazines, and came out on to the beaten earth sidewalk.

Slackly, she strolled over to the main entrance of the hotel and had a message sent up to Martin's room. He came down at once and crossed to where she sat, in a corner of the main lounge.

"I'm so glad you managed it," he said. "This has been one of the longest days of my life."

"And mine." She took a cigarette from his packet and steadied it at his match. "Been working?"

"Trying to." He shifted his seat. "I'll never produce anything in this place. You saw Paterson?"

"Yes. It was no good."

As she inhaled, Martin noticed the nerve twitching in her cheek.

"Was he unpleasant?"

"Not . . . particularly."

"You look rather down, Tess."

"I am, a bit. I woke with a head this morning and it hasn't cleared yet."

"Through me? Oh, Tess."

His devotion and tenderness grated. She could not bear to look at his fine-drawn features, the mouth to which pain came too easily. She took one more pull at the cigarette and squashed it out in a misshapen brass ash-tray strapped to the arm of her chair.

"I can't stay, Martin, and I may not come in again this week."

"May I come to your house?"

"Not yet. I'll get in touch with you."

He walked out with her and up to the bookshop where the jeep was parked. When she was sitting at the wheel he spoke through the window.

"Tess, I've been making enquiries. There's a small farm for sale the other side of town. I could buy it for a down payment of six hundred."

"Why don't you?" she said dully.

"I can't till you've been over it."

Her eyes filmed. She switched on the ignition and thumbed the starter. "I'm not choosing your future home for you, Martin. You must please yourself. Good-bye."

As she moved off his face was reflected in the square mirror attached to the windscreen; pale and tight with torment of his own making. How had she come to be mixed up with such a man?

But as Parsburg receded, so did Martin. Suppose Dave stayed away again this evening? Suppose he was waiting for a move from her? But that was not his way. Unwittingly, she had humiliated him, and he was making her pay for it. If she crawled to him — and every sinew shrank from such a course — nothing would ever again be clear between them. She had to sit back till the parting began to punish him, but be ready with a smile and arms wide, for his return.

It took her fully thirty seconds to realize that the oncoming car in the distance was Dave's. In a reflex action her foot switched to the brake, and her breathing accelerated. The smile had already begun on her lips and her eyes were misting with the peculiar delight of this moment.

Everyone knew everyone else on this road, and he couldn't help but recognize the jeep. He was approaching fast, but it would be like him to jerk to a sudden halt, as if he had stopped against his saner judgment. He was very near. She pressed the brake the whole way . . . and then it was over. A speeding black shape with Dave staring ahead as if the road was clear, and his trail of dust sweeping across the veld with the wind.

In a mental paralysis Tess gazed at the thinning dust. Her knuckles gleamed white on the wheel.

Presently, from a long way off she heard her own voice: "Oh, God. Where do I go from here?"

During the next few days Tess felt herself sinking into a lethargy which was hardly more tolerable than suffering; she had never reacted spontaneously to negative conditions. Stagnation was loathsome and to be avoided at all costs. Yet her situation was ideal for it.

Isolated at the house, she spoke to no one but Katie or August. Another prospective buyer did inspect the rooms, but he was dealing with the attorney and his interest in Tess ceased when she retreated behind a journal and ignored him. After he had gone she wished she had accepted the invitation in his eyes and used him as a companion for a few hours. His masculine aroma had awakened a bitter nostalgia for Dave's smoky fragrance, and left her shivering with pain till the blankness enwrapped her once more.

She became accustomed to hearing the sedan slow down to turn the corner, and she knew, without watching, that Dave never moved his head as he sped past. This thing would be so much easier to bear if their houses were far apart.

Through Katie, who got it from her sons, Tess heard that an offer had been made for the store and negotiations started. "*Baas* Paterson" had given orders for a split-pole fence to be erected on three sides of the plot, cutting it off entirely from the citrus farm,

75

and one of the stipulations in the sale provided for the complete repainting of the buildings, and cleaning up of the lawns and yard.

Martin wrote twice, begging to be allowed to come over, and to the second letter she briefly replied that she would drop in at the hotel one day soon.

A fortnight dragged by. Then one morning she went to the store for some cotton. Mrs. Marais was there, supporting her large bosom on the counter and laboriously scribbling her requirements on the note-pad.

Mrs. Marais tapped her crooked white teeth with the pencil. "I think that is all, Jacob. You will send them before midday?" She threw a short-sighted glance over her shoulder. "Good morning, Tess. We don't often see you now."

Tess murmured something.

"And how is the young man — Mr. Cramer?"

"Quite well. He's living in Parsburg."

"We used to joke about him, Piet and I. He was a good boy, jealous of you with the *baas*."

Tess forced a smile. "Silly of him."

"I wouldn't say that." Mrs. Marais' mouth quirked archly. "We thought he had good reason. The *baas* has been kind to you since you heard the bad news about your father. He's a generous man — to all of us."

"Has he raised Piet's wages?"

"A little, but the bonus was the welcome surprise. And he said that if the farm is in good shape when he comes back there will be another bonus. Think of that!"

With fingers gripped in upon her palms, Tess echoed: "When he comes back? So he's going to Lokola, after all?"

"By now he's half-way there. He left the day before yesterday. Surely he said good-bye to you as he passed?"

"No. No, he didn't." Her teeth were tight with the effort of control. "Possibly I was out. How long will he be gone?"

"Eight or ten weeks. He's locked up the house and handed the key to Mr. Arnold."

Somehow, Tess dragged herself free and got back to her dining-room. Shakily, she lit a cigarette and flicked the match out of the window. This would pass — it must. It was the suddenness that hurt like a knife twisted in her heart. Of course he had gone to Lokola, and it was her own fault that she hadn't gone with him. She should have submerged her pride; there were ways a woman could do it without too much loss of face. In any case, pride was a fraud when it parted two people who were in love with each other.

Her thoughts paused, hollowly. Was Dave in love with her? Could a man wound so cruelly a woman he loved? He had packed up and gone, put three or four thousand miles between them without so much as a gesture of farewell. What did he intend her to learn from that? That he would have no difficulty in getting along without her, that the marriage proposal had been solely for her benefit and relinquished by him with relief? She wouldn't believe it.

Yet there were other, more deadly implications. In a couple of months the store would belong to someone else and Tess would be forced to leave Zinto. He would return to find her removed to Parsburg, and well out of the path of temptation.

Eight or ten weeks and no hope of a letter from him. She might write to him: "I love you, Dave. Please send word that you forgive me." But what good would it do? Even by air the postal delays to the tropics were enormous. A letter might not reach him for a fortnight, and if he replied by return, which was problematical, a month would pass before she could hear from him. A month of anguished hope and despair. Besides, his departure had been so deliberate, so coldly brutal. She could imagine him tearing the letter across and hating her for reminding him of the thing he had determined to forget.

Perhaps putting her from his mind would prove impossible; need of her might bring him home sooner . . . But no, not Dave. Into her mad refusal to hurt Martin he had read belittlement of himself, and humiliation happened to be a quality he could not live with. If only he'd given her the chance to climb down. What did she care about Martin? True, there had been a time, not so long ago, when he had stirred in her a protective pity, but that was before he threatened the relationship between Dave and herself. Now, she felt nothing for him but a deadly distaste. She never wanted to see him again.

Yet it was impossible to wish that Dave had never entered her life. Back in the house she recalled ecstasies in his arms, and trembled with the terrible longing to feel him close again. There was no pain so grinding as this; no loss so shattering as that which comes precipitately upon the awakening and fulfilment of love.

Tess made some coffee and drank it with a splash of brandy. She lit another cigarette and discarded it half-way through. Her head was floating with hunger and as the sun waned she felt cold and bloodless. She paced the veranda, walked round the paths between sere grasses, and came back to find Martin poking his head into the hall. At her step he turned.

"Tess!" he exclaimed. And then, "Oh, Tess darling," in a tender, suffering voice that touched her nerves with fire.

"What do you want?"

He stared, unbelieving. "My dear, what is it? You're unwell . . . or did I frighten you?"

She made a harsh, breaking sound of laughter. "Frighten me? You? That's nearly funny. You couldn't frighten anyone, Martin. Why have you come here?"

"I couldn't bear not to," he said simply. "You look so . . . ravaged. Tell . . . tell me what's happened."

Her teeth snapped hard. "Yes, I'll tell you. Dave Paterson and I were in love . . . he wanted to marry me. I tried to postpone marriage, for your sake . . . because I hadn't the courage to hurt you." Heedless of his white, stricken face, she went on rapidly: "Dave demanded that I never see you again . . . but I wouldn't promise. So he's gone away, and when he returns there'll be someone new at the store, and I shall be safely out of his way for ever. That's what happened, Martin! You've merely crippled my life, destroyed the loveliest thing that ever came into it.

Now do you understand why I can't look at you without loathing?"

He had fallen back against the veranda post. His throat worked but he made no sound. Her fury had abated, leaving her pale and spent.

"You'd better get out, Martin, and stay out. You and I have no use for each other any more."

"You love Paterson," he whispered. "I thought you might. But if he can leave you on my account he doesn't love you. I know you're stronger than I am, more balanced and sensible. In time you'll get over wanting Dave, but I shall go on wanting you for the rest of my life. Tess—"

"Please go, Martin."

"But when can I see you again?"

"I've told you," she said with icy viciousness. "I'm finished with you. I don't care what you do or where you go, so long as we never meet again."

She turned indoors and left him there, slumped against the rusting iron post. She lay on her bed in a dreadful apathy of weakness and misery, and after a while she slipped into an exhausted doze.

A few days later the buyer of the store came over to make arrangements about moving in. He turned out to be the man who had begged for an option and been refused. When the attorney informed him that an offer had been received, the man had decided to cable his prospective bride, and as a consequence he had raised the figure by two hundred and fifty, and made up his mind to have the place ready for when she arrived. Money, he explained, would be a little tight at first. Was Miss Bentley willing to quote him an all-in price for the furnishings as the house stood? He and his wife could replace them gradually.

Tess shrugged. She didn't care what he did. Slackly, she agreed to allow a painter from Parsburg access to the house; she accepted a cheque to cover both furniture and jeep, and promised to get the boys working on the garden.

The day before Tess was due to depart, Cath Arnold came over, alone. She rested on the gate, her glance admiringly sweeping the renovated bungalow.

"My word, I never thought it could ever gleam like that. And the flat lawns! I bet it twists your heart a bit to think of someone else living here."

"Not much, to be candid," Tess told her. "I've no people — nothing to keep me at Zinto."

"In any case, you've come out well financially, haven't you? They tell me the store sold for over five thousand. What are you planning for the future?"

"Nothing, yet. Tomorrow I go to the coast for a holiday. After that I may join my brothers in England."

"Shan't we be seeing you up here any more?"

"I'm not sure. Coming in for a drink?"

"Sorry, but I mustn't stay that long. I came to invite you to use our spare bedroom for a week or two, but if you've already booked at the coast . . ."

Tess hadn't, but neither had she any desire to live with neighbours. There was only one thing she needed to learn from Cath.

Offhandedly she said: "Everard is managing Zinto at the moment, isn't he? Have you heard from Dave?"

"We had an airmail from him yesterday, merely half a dozen lines to say that he'd arrived in Lokola and found the place unchanged. Everard will be sending him a report at the end of the month." Cath paused. "I believe it was all for the best that Dave didn't care enough for Mariella. He's not an ordinary type of man. She'd have developed into a drag on him and made them both unhappy."

"Probably."

The silence which followed had a vague unrest. Conventionally, Cath ended it.

"Look here, Tess, you'll keep in touch with us, won't you? Even if we haven't been close friends, we've been neighbours for a long time. We'll be interested to hear all about you, and I'll send you the local news. Hazel will be keen to hear from you, so do send her a postcard now and then."

"I will."

Cath had got back into the old car. Her head poked out. "You did hear about Martin Cramer, I suppose?"

"Nothing recent. Is he still at the hotel?"

"No, my dear. He's vanished, but left his bags and things in his room. Caused quite an upheaval for a couple of days. The police were working on it but had to give up for lack of evidence. I always said there was something uncanny about that young man."

Walking up towards the house after Cath had driven away, Tess pondered, without feeling, upon Martin's disappearance. Instinctively, she was sure that he had not entered the hotel since she had sent him away from Zinto. It would be in character for him to have taken his car as far as he could in the direction opposite from Parsburg. He was simply trying, as she intended to try tomorrow, to run away from pain.

CHAPTER SEVEN

DAVE had been right about Lourenço Marques. Portuguese East Africa was an experience in which, had her mood been gay and unfettered, she would have delighted for a while and ultimately have tired of. As she had expected, it was almost like living in a separate and vastly more colourful continent. The mosaic pavements, the Praça Sete de Março and its bandstand surrounded by little wine tables, the casinos, the lovely Polana Beach and all the rest of the expensive sophistication of the place were excitingly different from anything she had known or heard about.

With a Johannesburg family who happened to be holiday-making at the same hotel, Tess did the usual rounds of the city and surrounding districts. She went up the river at Marracuene and saw the hippo skirmishing, walked in the Vasco da Gama gardens and admired the Portuguese-style gateway which guards the entrance to the museum. At night she danced a little, witnessed the floor shows and lost a large number of escudos in the casinos.

When her friends returned to Johannesburg, Tess decided to move on to Durban, where the language was mainly English and she could read the familiar newspapers. But Durban had even less to offer her bruised spirit than had Lourenço Marques.

She spent a few days at East London, and passed on to Port Cranston, where, as was becoming her habit, she took up residence at one of the best hotels overlooking the sea.

Dave had been gone six weeks. Three weeks from now she would take the train to Parsburg, and meanwhile she would play desperately to shorten the days.

It was hunger for companionship which made her accept lifts from the other residents along the Esplanade into town. Invariably they invited her to do a cinema with them, or to bathe, or to drive out to one of the guest farms for tea. And it was the same feeling which impelled her to notice the couple who sat at the next table in the long dining-room, though she rather had the impression that they had smiled at her a few times before she was entirely conscious of their proximity. Because they were of opposite sexes and near ages, she presumed they were husband and wife.

He was good-looking in an ascetic fashion, darkish and long-featured with a gently smiling mouth and hazel eyes. Tess put his age at about thirty, and the woman's at twenty-eight. Obviously, this brown-haired, brown-eyed goddess was a career-woman and exceptionally strong-willed. The wonder was that the man hadn't succumbed to her domination.

One evening, just after dinner, Tess learned why. The native boy who usually pulled wide the heavy swing door for her was missing. Someone said quickly, "Allow me," and there was the darkish man, inclining his head at her with a charming smile as he held back the door, to permit Tess and his table companion to pass through.

In the wide corridor from the dining-room to the main lounge, Tess found herself between the couple.

"Have coffee with us, won't you?" the woman suggested.

"You take so much for granted, Julie," he said. "Miss Bentley hasn't the least notion who we are. She's new to the town."

"Are you famous?" asked Tess.

"Merely well known in Port Cranston. My sister is a doctor, and I'm Richard Barnwell, best known as my father's son."

"Barnwells, the antique dealers in Main Street?"

"Exactly. My father started the business and when he died it became mine." His expression had a touch of self-mockery. "Barnwells began as an exchange mart in a wooden shack on the water-front, fifty years ago. Today we're known as the only dealers in genuine antiques in this part of the country. Where will you sit?"

She chose a chair and waited till the Indian waiter had poured coffee and moved away to serve others, before saying, with a smile: "It doesn't do to sneer at one's beginnings or to throw them out as a challenge to other people. My father set up as a trader in a native reserve about thirteen years ago. The district expanded and more white people came in, so we did very well. My two brothers are at universities in England, and at the moment I'm a person of modest but adequate means. That kind of thing is common in a young country."

"We wondered about you," Julia Barnwell threw out bluntly. "Even took the trouble to ask who you were. A girl staying alone in an hotel is uncommon, and you, if I may say so, are very attractive. Did your mother have that silver-gilt hair?"

"No, hers was tawny, and my father's darker."

"I told you so, Richard! The true white-blonde is invariably a phenomenon." She turned to the hovering waiter, lifted a written message from his tray, and read it. "Oh, damn. Another call. I'll see you both later."

She went off smartly, her tailored dress swinging. Richard got out his cigarette-case.

"Don't let Julie's outspokenness disturb you. She did her studying among men and developed that line as a sort of defence. No doubt it helps in her work, too." He struck a match and held it to her cigarette. "You don't mind our curiosity about you?"

"Not a bit. I'm curious about you, too. Why, if you're Port Cranston people, are you living in an hotel?"

"We have a house at the back of the town. Julie is soon going to marry another doctor, but before they can practise there together extensive alterations to the rooms are necessary. She drives up daily to the surgery and to watch progress, but we both find it less wearing to sleep and eat here." He inhaled and flicked out the match. Quietly he added, "Why are you alone?"

A slight premonitory chill crept up her spine. She looked down at the gay spotted hem of the cream linen dress swathing her calves. "My father died, the store was sold and I discovered myself possessed of over three thousand, so I decided to have my first real holiday."

"How old are you?"

"Twenty."

"Awfully young." He said it as if in answer to a private doubt. "I've watched you, perhaps more than I should. You're unhappy about something."

"Aren't we all?" she returned lightly. "You're not particularly radiant yourself, but I don't suppose you spill your troubles to everyone you meet."

"I haven't any — only a general dissatisfaction with things as they are." He leaned back. "Sorry to have probed just now. How long are you staying?"

"About three weeks."

"Fine. Will you go out with me one evening?"

"Thanks," she said. "I'd like to."

Tess thought that Richard Barnwell would leave her alone after that. Something in her appearance had caught his fancy but the follow-up had disappointed him, which couldn't be helped. But next morning he half-rose from his breakfast-table to greet her, and when he came in at five-thirty he immediately sought her out and ordered sundowners. Later, he insisted that she dine at his table, and when Julie showed up, he told her point-blank that he was taking Miss Bentley to a show in the Town Hall.

Richard could not have been termed a commonplace man. He had travelled in search of education and *objets d'art,* had helped to launch a mission in Swaziland, and was a respected councillor of Port Cranston.

Yet with him Tess found little necessity to dissimulate. Probably the fact of hardly caring what he thought of her had much to do with her ease in his company. She was as readily quiet as talkative, and if she preferred an hour at her bedroom window watching the fresco of palms against the heaving Indian Ocean, she did not hesitate to tell him so.

Her complete indifference vexed and intrigued Richard, the more so as his sister had taken to referring to Tess as his "fair nymph." The juggernaut quality in Julie had never rasped him so much as it did now, when she teased him heavily and mercilessly about Tess Bentley, and told him he had better work fast if the girl was here for so short a stay. After all, she reminded him, he had already had one wife. . . .

It was many months since Richard had reflected upon the fiasco of his marriage; one doesn't dwell too often upon the painful mistakes in life, particularly when the brief space of a year had encompassed their inception and sudden conclusion. In the two years since the divorce he had realized why he had married Robina, and the reasons for the collapse of the partnership. Robina's surface had been insidiously feminine but at heart she had been too like Julie. She had scoffed at his chivalry and the positive need in him to protect his own woman, shrugged away his desire for children and taunted him with being too gentle a lover.

When his memories had taken him that far, Richard jibbed. It didn't do to dig up the grim bones of that year, the indignities which incompatibility heaps upon the sensitive.

From the moment when Tess's whitish curls and smooth tan had drawn his gaze to her table, Richard had rigidly considered her as just another lovely; at this season of the year the resort was peppered with them, though they were invariably accompanied by parents or youthful husbands. The shadow in the very blue eyes rather tilted at his judgment, and her total unconcern with her effect upon others posed another question. Nor was she pretty in the currently accepted sense. Unusual, of course, and slightly boyish in manner, but with potential sweetness and humour in the wide, red mouth. Not a vestige of Robina's opulence, yet her figure was one to hold the eye.

On her last Saturday they did some surf-riding. For Tess it was an initiation into an exhilarating new sport, and after it she flopped down upon her bathrobe, panting explosively. Richard, on his elbow beside her, watched her breathing lose its depth and her thick lashes lying over the faint hollows below her eyes.

Presently he asked, "What will you do in Parsburg, Tess?"

Her eyelids flickered. "I have to settle final details with the lawyer and pick up my mail."

"You've nothing to keep you there . . . have you?"

"I don't know."

Richard slipped right back, with a hand under his head. "I'd hate to lose touch with you."

"Been nice, hasn't it?" she said remotely.

"Too nice," he answered, his tone studiously ordinary. "You've made me wish I could undo the last three years of my life. Tess, does the fact that I've been divorced affect your conception of me?"

"I've never thought about it. A good many of us have something we'd rather hide, but divorce is so blatant that the wronged party can't help but suffer publicly. I suppose an unhappy marriage, even a brief one, changes a man quite a lot . . . but I didn't know you before it."

"If only you had," he said.

She didn't remind him that at seventeen she was still a student at Grahamstown; in fact she didn't even think of it. The palms in the orderly lawns which backed the beach rustled with a sudden strong breeze which washed gratefully over her golden skin. She had no desire to move, no wish for anything beyond her present mental and physical lassitude.

"I could take you to Parsburg," he suggested, "and knock around there for a few days. I haven't explored that district."

"There's nothing to explore. It's just a fair sized *dorp* surrounded by farms. Flat country, except for the little Witbergs, and so dry that the grass is mostly white and the red-hot pokers grey. Apart from Zinto, I've no affection for the neighbourhood."

"You said that Zinto is an orange farm. Where citrus grows you find moisture."

"There's the Zinto River bordering the property."

"Then . . . may I drive you up, Tess?"

"No," she said, and to soften the sudden sharpness in her voice, added, "your setting is Port Cranston, Richard — your gardens and large house, the baroque furniture, Florentine lamps and fine pictures. You'd loathe the veld town atmosphere of Parsburg and couldn't help but be contemptuous of the people there. Oh yes," she went on as a sound from him warned her of an interjection, "you have the warmest admiration for the farmers — backbone of South Africa and all that — but you and they wouldn't mix."

"I mix with you!" She heard him move up again on to his elbow and knew that his gaze upon her face missed nothing. "You're different from any woman I've ever known. At first I couldn't believe you had grown up in the backveld; you were too intelligent, too knowledgeable, too utterly unselfconscious among townsfolk. Then it occurred to me that some kind of experience had made you impervious for the time being, and . . . well, I suspected a disappointing love affair. Somehow, that . . . and your somewhat alien background brought you close to me. I can't let you take a train straight out of my life."

"I may come back — some time."

Richard was silent for so long that she drew the robe round her and sat up. He still leaned on his side, and she saw that his cheek-bones had darkened with blood.

He said, "For the present I must be content with that, but I'm going to miss you, Tess."

The following Tuesday he drove Tess and her luggage to catch the north-bound express. He bought her some magazines, cigarettes and a tin of chocolates, and strolled up and down the platform with her.

Sirens created a commotion. Richard put her into her booked seat, smiled and pressed her shoulder.

"Send me a wire when you're coming back," he said. "I'll meet you."

CHAPTER EIGHT

PARSBURG had shrunk and become rather dingy. After the dense greenness of the coast the trees looked stunted and gasping, the palms sere, and the gardens pathetic little patches of colour in the everlasting pall of pinkish dust. Fleetingly, because it was unwise as yet to bring Dave too vividly to mind, she recalled his assertion that she wouldn't think much of Zinto if she had known other places.

It was not till Tess had booked her hotel room and was signing the register that she remembered Martin. Pen poised, she asked, "Mr. Cramer isn't here now, is he?"

The manager's wife first stared, then became animated. "Of course! You're Miss Bentley of the Zinto store — hardly recognized you, my dear, and in any case I seldom have local residents staying here. Haven't you heard?"

"About what?"

"Mr. Cramer. He disappeared and left his things behind. My husband got worried and called in the police, but they couldn't discover anything . . ."

Extraordinary how completely Martin had receded from her existence, thought Tess. The woman was still talking.

". . . not too good for the reputation of the hotel, so we were glad when they dropped enquiries. A month passed and we decided the whole thing had blown over. Then there was a startling case in the *Parsburg Advertiser*. A native had given information to the police that a young white man had bought a hut in one of the kraals and was living in it. Who should it turn out to be but our Mr. Cramer. He was brought to court, and pleaded that he hadn't known that living with natives was against the law."

"Oh," said Tess faintly. "Did they . . . sentence him?"

"No, two doctors certified that he was too sick to go to prison. He was extradited — isn't that the word? The police came here again about ten days ago, and packed and labelled his cases. They were sent to a hospital in Switzerland."

"Oh, God." Tess murmured it shakily, like the prelude to a prayer.

She scrawled an illegible signature and turned at once to follow the boy who waited with her luggage in the tiny, old-fashioned lift.

In her small, dusty room she stood with her back against the door, fighting down a dreadful dizziness. In a moment she moved to an old wicker chair and subsided into it, eyes closed.

Stupid to blame herself. She wasn't responsible for Martin's actions. Come to that, she had had as much reason to behave abnormally as he had, but she had done the sensible thing: gone away for a holiday to give circumstances a chance of improving. Except, of course, that she had grounds for believing that Dave loved her, whereas Martin was a man without hope. She hadn't been fair to him, but through Martin she had behaved even more badly to Dave.

By morning's glaring sunlight, Martin faded a little. She had come to Parsburg with a purpose, the first step being to find out whether Dave had yet returned to Zinto. Perhaps the simplest means would be to call on the bookseller who supplied him with newspapers and periodicals; almost certainly he would renew his order at once.

After breakfast she crossed to the post-office to collect her mail. A quick glance through the half-dozen envelopes, and her hopes, which had wishfully begun a cautious soaring, dropped back to zero. There were two letters from Gerald and one from Alan, some bulky accounts sheets from the lawyer, two pages of close script from the Johannesburg matron she had met in Lourenço Marques and a couple of trade circulars announcing still more ways in which to entice the natives to yield up their pay. She tore up the latter, and slipped the other four into her bag.

Resolutely she went to the neat bookshop. The elderly woman assistant came forward, disguised a quirk of surprise at the familiar figure in an unfamiliar and beautifully simple linen suit, and smiled a welcome.

"Good morning, Tess. We thought you'd left these parts for good. Can I help you?"

"I'll take the *Advertiser* and a couple of magazines. Yes, those will do." Tess paused, leafing through a book which lay on the stand at her side. Without looking up, she asked, "Is the new store owner one of your customers?"

"He wasn't at first — till his wife came. She opened an account with us right away. A nice, homely sort of woman."

"I'm glad. I suppose Zinto is back to usual now that Mr. Paterson is home?"

"Is he home?" The woman was perplexed and eager. "When did he arrive?"

"I was guessing. I only got in myself last night."

"Then I think your guess must be wrong, Tess. Mrs. Arnold of Inchfaun was in here the other day and she didn't mention Mr. Paterson at all. Yet she told me herself about a month ago that Mr. Arnold is looking after Zinto and that she would let me know the date of Mr. Paterson's return, so that he shouldn't miss his periodicals. Will that be all? Thank you."

So! Tess came out into the sunshine and drew a long, unsteady breath. What now? A casual visit to Cath Arnold in search of the latest information? Would it strike the Arnolds as odd that she should part with a large taxi fare in order to spend a friendly hour with them? Cath was as capable as the next woman of sorting the important features from a seemingly innocuous conversation, but Tess was in a condition to risk a good deal. She wouldn't hear the gossip, anyway, and only the meanest-souled woman would repeat it to Dave.

According to Mrs. Marais, Dave had intended being away from eight to ten weeks. This was his ninth week, so he might be on the plane for Johannesburg. Supposing she learned from Cath that he was due home within a few days, what could she do about it? Very little, it would seem. Previously, Dave had come often to town, to the bank or the post-office, to the seed merchant or the co-operative depot. He had also made friends at the Sports Club. She knew him well enough to be certain that he would find out where she was staying, and if he still smarted a messenger would be sent daily to Parsburg, and Dave would reserve his social calls till the evening, when there might be little chance of an encounter.

And, of course, Dave did still smart, or he would have written her, however briefly and cynically. But that aspect Tess firmly thrust away, for subconsciously she was convinced that even Dave could not go on wounding her when he became aware of her regret and willingness to atone. Perhaps — her heart leapt — he would hear about Martin and realize that she had obeyed his will after all. He would hurry to her and take her into his arms, curse himself for a savage-tempered brute.

She had come to a standstill beneath a cement portico. Blindly, she gazed at the wide entrance to an office block. Oh yes — the lawyer. Might as well get that over. She mounted the white stone steps to the upper floor, walked along the corridor and automatically turned left and into the small office where a typist presided. Five minutes later she had passed through to the lawyer's sanctum.

She listened, not very intently, to his explanations regarding the account, and wrote a cheque to cover the debt.

"I have transferred an amount of three thousand four hundred to your brother Alan in London," he said, "and sent Gerald a full statement of the financial transactions. I presume you will no longer wish me to act for you?"

"Seeing that we've gone out of business," she shrugged, "there's nothing for you to do. But tell me something. How did we really come out — we Bentleys? What did the business and stock fetch, apart from the property?"

"It's easy enough to work out. The buildings and land were valued at two thousand six hundred."

"Was Mr. Paterson told of the valuation?"

"It was he who authorized it, when he made the deed of gift. I gave him the figure and he was very pleased. I remember him saying you deserved it."

"How kind."

"In just a few months Mr. Paterson has increased the value of the property by about ten per cent," the lawyer said, "though his instructions are to sell at the amount he paid."

She sat motionless for a minute. Then, with desperate deliberation, she got out cigarettes and matches. She lit up and blew a cloud of smoke, folded the few papers which rested on her side of the desk and inserted them into her bag.

"So he's . . . giving up Zinto?"

"Exactly, and I already have someone interested. It won't even be necessary to advertise the farm or to put it into the hands of an estate agent." The man was mentally rubbing his hands.

Carefully, Tess enquired, "When is Mr. Paterson coming here?"

"He isn't coming. We've been corresponding about this matter and he is leaving the sale entirely in my hands. It's my belief that very soon I shall be in a position to send him the documents for signature, and after that the transfer will take a matter of weeks."

"You mean . . . he's never coming this way again?"

The man laughed good-humouredly. "That is his intention. I'm afraid others don't take to our countryside as we do. In his opinion Zinto is dried-up and godforsaken."

"Will he remain in Lokola?"

"I rather think he will. There's a mine in which he owns a share, and within days of his arrival at the place he was asked to give technical assistance at a government mine in the district. Men like Paterson are soon snapped up for good positions in the tropics."

"What about the car he left in a garage in Johannesburg?"

"I've sold it for him."

"And the house furniture?"

"It goes with the property."

Tess paused, willing herself to get up and go. But she had to ask it. "Has Mr. Paterson ever mentioned the store in his letters?"

"He did in the first one. Apparently Mr. Arnold wrote him that you had moved out and he wanted reassurance from me that all the monies had been correctly apportioned between you and Alan, and paid out."

"That was all?"

The lawyer nodded. "Are you settling in Parsburg?"

"No, I'm not." Tess was surprised to find that her legs would hold her. She went to the door. "Good-bye, and thanks for all you've done for my brothers and me."

She walked back to the hotel and took the stairs to her room. Without hesitation she dragged out her trunk and began to fold into it the dresses she had hung out last night. Once or twice she tried to blink the ache from her eyes and to swallow on the burning obstruction in her throat. This was worse than if he had died, this purposeful severing of every link with which he considered past folly. Well, at least she had the slap in the face to remember him by. And the pain would have to lessen. It couldn't possibly go on tearing her apart like this.

The midnight train from Greenside carried Tess away for good. She sat up through the dark hours fighting down the bitterness and the shattering sense of hopelessness and loss. The sun rose above the thick green trees of the coastal belt and washed in lurid streams across an ultramarine back-cloth. She refused breakfast but drank some coffee.

At eight o'clock the train pulled in to Port Cranston. Tess had her belongings transferred to a taxi and directed the driver to the hotel. They passed along the Esplanade; to the left stretched the line of date palms in close-cropped grass and the white beach lapped by a slumbrous blue ocean.

The taxi curved up the drive and was paid off. Two native boys dealt with the luggage. Tess mounted the steps to the elegant porch and gazed dully into the eyes of Richard Barnwell.

For a moment neither spoke. All his attention was concentrated upon her incredible lack of colour and the smudges under her eyes, her entire appearance of defeat and grief.

Instead of the swift exclamation of pleasure which had risen to his lips, he said gently: "You've travelled all night. You must be very tired, Tess."

"I feel ready to drop dead," she said unemotionally. "In fact, I wish I could."

BOOK II

CHAPTER ONE

A MOUNTAIN range smothered in giant ferns, the clefts packed tight with wild banana and tall, stringy rubber trees, meandered between the coastline and Lokola. Streams spouted high up in the green faces, joined in a foaming waterfall to form an inland river which, before it had channelled a dozen miles, seeped out on each side into the tangled jungle, creating a formidable swamp which had so far proved an unbridgable barrier to railway construction. The ores mined in the region had to travel across country on a narrow-gauge track to meet the main line.

The white residents of Lokola numbered fourteen, and of these nine lived in the sedate houses at the station proper, and the other five dwelt in four oblong mud houses with thatched roofs which had been set up in a small clearing about half a mile to the north. One of the four houses was Dave Paterson's.

Years ago, when he had first come to Lokola, Dave had been allotted a splendid white house alongside the district officer's. But he had quickly tired of the stilted atmosphere and monotonous parties patronized by the same few people; more to his taste was a stroll up the track for a game of cards and an exchange of yarns with Walton, the palm-oil trader, and Brigham, who at that time had no particular occupation beyond scratching below the surface of the red-brown earth for signs of copper and tin. Redding wasn't a bad chap, either, so long as one veiled one's curiosity as to the source of his ivory supplies.

When he had driven away from Lokola presumably for good, he thought he had abandoned his dwelling to damp rot and the swift disintegration which attends anything that is uncared for in such places. But Walton, that far-seeing, gentle, sly comrade, had ordered a weekly cleaning and airing of the place. Upon his return, Dave had found his house and furniture much as he had left them, except for the heaps of ant-dust inside the cupboards, a sagging thatch and several rotten floorboards. And Luke Walton was there, pleased and unsurprised, his long rangy body propped against the door-frame while he watched Dave's cursory inspection of the couple of rooms.

Luke had said calmly: "You can borrow some of my blankets and linen and china till yours come through from the coast. I expect you've ordered supplies?"

"Not yet, but I will."

Luke had given a satisfied sigh. "I don't want to know why you're back, Dave — but I'm glad you are. It hasn't been the same here without you."

Dave had nodded across at the tidy bed and the clean lamp on the bedside table. "Looks as if you were expecting me."

"Well, you wouldn't sell up the tin workings and often your letters sounded sort of savage. I just couldn't see you growing roots among orange trees — not unless you picked up a wife and decided to go in for a family."

"Forget it, Walt," had been the brief reply.

Luke had promptly obeyed. He gave the news. Brigham still lived next door with the Malay, but since the woman had had a baby she was not so well and was seldom seen; probably she was again pining for her own people. Redding had done a lunatic thing only a month ago — married a woman he had run into at Freetown and brought her here to live with him; a dark, good-looking creature who had obviously used him as a get-out from some mess or other. She despised poor old Redding because he was fifty and hadn't quite the polish of a gentleman; she hated Brigham for a "fat, degenerate toad," and tolerated Luke Walton because he himself was tolerant and kind.

"Her name is Avia," he ended. "God knows where she originated or what she's been through in her twenty-eight years, but one thing is certain — she hooked Redding because she was hard up, that's all. What I can't get at is why she didn't marry someone working in Freetown and grab herself a gay time."

Dave had made a disinterested comment. Later, when he had met Avia Redding and heard Brigham's ribald view of the marriage, he concluded, still without interest, that the woman had been married before and that possibly her union with Redding was bigamous. One continually came up against the unconventional in equatorial Africa.

News came through that the orange farm was sold, and later his bank advised that the purchase money had been paid in. Within four months of shaking off the pungent-sweet scent of Zinto, he was back where he had been two years ago . . . except that now he was without any objective beyond the expert handling of his machinery and squads of natives.

Gradually, he revised his estimate of Avia Redding; there couldn't be a lot of harm in a woman who succeeded in being a fairly good wife to someone for whom she had an undeniable contempt. Her tropic pallor, her age and obvious sophistication, placed her in a familiar category. Dave accepted her story that she had come out from England five years ago to teach and nurse at a native mission and had rocked the settlement to its worm-eaten foundations by marrying a Belgian seaman. Sheer filthy luck, of course, that the man should succumb to a fever and Avia find herself alone, penniless and ostracized. She had been tossing up whether to return to an unpalatably strenuous life in London or to offer her services to a hospital in Freetown when Francis Redding had suggested a more comfortable way out.

"Do you blame me?" she once asked Dave, challengingly.

"No — so long as you've the sense to realize that this can't last. I give you a year at most with Redding."

Avia had smiled and slanted at him a smoky glance. "That will be enough. You underestimate your own magnetism, Dave. I'm already curious about you."

"Curiosity won't get you anywhere," he had told her bluntly.

She had shrugged, undismayed. "We're both civilized, and I've learned the value of being a white woman in a masculine red hell. I've also heard rumours about you. Tut, tut, David."

Avia certainly possessed an undemanding and rather subtle charm. Experience had taught her restraint and

97

the incalculable worth of a cool brain, however torrid the atmosphere; and where her deepest desires were at stake her patience was infinite.

Christmas passed without festivity. By day a hot, dry wind swept down from the desert, lessening the humidity but spoiling the usually cool evenings. No one sought his bed till after midnight and by five in the morning everybody was astir. The few hours within a mosquito net were a wakeful, sweating nightmare. Legions of insects swarmed through the clearing. Brigham went down with malaria; so did Avia Redding.

That January was the worst Dave had ever experienced. Sickness among natives was continuous and severe. Atmospheric conditions played havoc with his plant and caused such wide rifts in the main road that work had to be abandoned till they were filled in and surfaced with chipped rocks. Brig remained too weak to superintend the tin mine, so Dave had to fit in a daily inspection of gear and give the half-breed foreman his instructions.

At the beginning of February there came a particularly annoying day. That morning the medical man had arrived for his periodical examination of the mine workers and discovered three incipient cases of sleeping sickness. The unfortunate victims had been instantly removed to a distant village where such patients were cared for, but the mere mention of the dread disease had reacted ruthlessly upon the rest of the boys. They were suddenly apathetic with resignation — to a degree only attainable by Africans, and several of them, pronounced fit by the doctor, developed alarming symptoms as soon as he had departed. Useless to assure them that their ills were imaginary. Dave had to think up some strong "medicine" in the way of pills and pep talk.

Aching with heat and long-drawn anger, he knocked off at four, took some tea and a bath, and flung himself into a long rattan lounger with a pillow behind his head and a pile of unanswered correspondence on the low table beside him. He read, occasionally pencilling a query into a margin or tearing a letter neatly into four. The peacefulness of this pleasant hour of the day stole over him. Flies and ants were becoming somnolent and mosquitoes had not yet set up their high-pitched singing. The boys were quiet, probably snoozing in their hut at the back, and tranquillity enveloped the other houses.

In fact, it was so still that he heard a car enter the Lokola station half a mile away. It reminded him that he ought to accept the district officer's invitation to dinner one night this week; there were one or two items he wanted cleared officially, and he had a hunch about the gun-running which would interest the D.O. He might send down a note as soon as one of the boys showed up to prepare his evening meal. It would be a change to discuss books and music and play a polite game of bridge after eight months of poker in dubious company.

A noise outside made Dave let down his legs so that he could lean sideways and look through the open doorway to the baked earth track. A car was advancing through the plantains, a small English saloon whose colour was obscured by thick red dust. At the first house it slowed, and as it reached Dave's it stopped. The car door was thrust open, a head emerged: a small golden face surmounted by a cap of whitish curls.

Very slowly, Dave got up. With an odd sort of deliberation he crossed the room, stepped into the porch and dropped down on to the track. The girl, slim and straight in leaf-green linen, turned and saw him. Her red lips widened into a cool, ironical smile.

"Mr. Paterson, I presume?"

"My God," he muttered. And then, with a swift effort at mockery, "Welcome to the jungle, Teresa."

Tess tilted back her head, the better to view the small white-washed dwelling with banana-leaf thatch which was interlaced at the ridge and spread down to cover a narrow veranda. Apart from the tan she was pale and the skin at her temples glistened with sweat, but her manner was calm and faintly bantering.

"So this is Lokola, your spiritual and material home. My imagination wasn't far out."

"Pity you didn't trust it," he returned grimly. "Seeing that you're here you'd better come in for a drink."

She preceded him. "Thanks. Your greeting isn't nearly as warm as the one I had from a man at the lower end of this hamlet. He told me yours was the second house and even offered to come up here with me. Still," she hesitated inside the door and let her glance rove over the plain teak and wicker furniture of the living-room, the loaded bookshelves and the couple of blue pillows on the lounger, "he doesn't know me as you do. The fact that last time we met you took a crack at my jaw might make this encounter somewhat delicate if we hadn't a great deal of common sense between us." Smiling, she sat down rather stiffly on the foot end of the lounger. "I haven't come to plague you, Dave — merely popped in for a sundowner in passing."

"That sounds plausible — a hundred miles from nowhere," he commented, pouring drinks. "Here, down this."

Tess took the glass and straightway swallowed half the contents. She shuddered and coughed.

"Lord . . . neat whisky! I haven't sunk to that yet."

"It's what you need, by the look of you." He drank from his own tumbler and leaned back on the dining-table, surveying her. "Who drove you in from the coast?"

"I drove myself . . . borrowed the car and set off like a pioneer at about ten-thirty this morning. I calculated that I'd reach here in time for lunch, but the mountains and swamps got in the way."

His mouth compressed. "So you're as crazy as ever. Didn't it occur to you to ask about the condition of the road?"

"You told me Lokola was a hundred miles inland, and I've managed rough journeys before."

"It's nearer a hundred and eighty miles by road and hellish going all the way. Did you get any lunch?"

"I found some wild bananas and tried a couple of half-ripe mangoes. They were terrible. I'm not hungry."

Dave took a sharp and furious breath. "D'you mind explaining?"

"My presence here?" She smoothed a small, bony brown hand over her skirt. "Since I finished at Zinto I've been travelling and seen most of the places we talked about. Lourenço Marques, the South African ports . . . I even touched down in Cairo on my way to England."

"So you did go to England?"

She nodded. "Three months ago, by plane. I might have stayed there if one of my brothers had had a home; or I'd have put up with hotel life a little longer if they'd needed me."

"They don't seem to have improved."

"I was only a kid when they went off, remember. Alan took me to the London theatres, and Gerald motored me through the Lake District; afterwards the three of us spent some days at Stratford-on-Avon."

"And having placated their consciences they once more abandoned you to your own devices." With rather less than his usual nonchalance, he offered cigarettes. "I still can't see why you had to come to Lokola."

"It's very simple." She tapped her cigarette on a thumb-nail. "I'm going back to the Cape. I think I shall settle in Port Cranston, and it's unlikely that I shall ever come north again. So, to get the most out of it, I'm travelling the slow way, by coastal boats. I've been to Lisbon and Madeira, and from Funchal I got a lift down as far as Dakar. I had quite a time at Dakar explaining away my lack of a visa, but the French were very helpful."

"You've done all this *alone?*"

Her grin, as she lifted her cigarette to his match, had a touch of defiance. "Amazing, isn't it?"

"Where's Cramer?"

Her smile faded right out. "Martin died in a Swiss hospital some months ago; he was given a couple of lines in a daily paper. The last time I saw him was the day I heard you had left Zinto for this spot."

"Oh." Dave was silent a moment; then he shifted his position and brought the subject back to the present. "When did you get to Cape Ricos?"

"Last night, and I re-embark tomorrow morning. Sorry to annoy you, Dave, but I really came more for my own sake than yours. I knew that colliding with me once more would hardly shake you fundamentally, but I wasn't completely sure about myself. I want to be whole-minded before I go back to Port Cranston."

Dave didn't answer. He flicked ash on to a tray, then moved across to the door which led to the kitchen.

"Are you there, Zula?"

A shuffle, and a thick voice replied, "Here, master."

"Get cold chop for two . . . quick."

Tess said, "I won't stay for dinner, but I wouldn't refuse a sandwich and some coffee."

"Why?" — tersely. "Got a date for the evening?"

"Yes, with a hundred and eighty miles of mud road. I'd like to be on the way before dark."

"I'll drive you."

"I don't want that." Her voice had risen with purpose. "I came here chiefly to pay a debt. Till recently I was a little too shattered to come round to it." She paused and opened the white bag which lay at her side. "I can't accept money for nothing, Dave. This is a cheque for two thousand six hundred, the value of the store property. Don't make the hackneyed gesture of tearing it up in front of me. If the cheque isn't paid in I shall draw the amount in cash and send it to you by registered post."

His gaze narrowed at the pink slip she had tossed on to the table. "Isn't it you who are making the trite gesture?"

"Possibly, but I can't go to another man with your money in the bank. Perhaps you'll feel happier about taking it if I tell you that the man I'm going to marry owns a prosperous business."

Dave's white teeth thoughtfully explored his lip for a few seconds. "Congratulations," he said, and mixed for himself a weak whisky and water. After which he added carelessly, "If you'd like to clean up before you eat, the bathroom is next to the kitchen."

"I . . . don't think I'll bother."

The slight, incongruous stammer seemed to hang between them. Dave's eyes sharpened.

"Take off your jacket, then, and relax."

"No . . . but I would be glad of that coffee, Dave."

"It's about ready — I can smell it." Irritably, he leaned over and shook up the pillow upon which his own head had rested. "For Pete's sake let go and lie down. You don't have to go on being merry and bright with me. I know all about that filthy trip, so don't try to kid me that your bones don't ache. I'd lay big money that your head's raging, too, and you feel some nausea. You're not accustomed to wet heat."

"Still masterful, aren't you?" she remarked, not moving from her rigidly upright posture on the lounger. A lock of hair had slipped forward over her brow, accentuating her look of youth. "Give me another cigarette, will you?"

But Dave didn't. He barked at the boy to hurry with the coffee, and went out himself to push in the trolley. Expertly, he filled a cup with black liquid, sugared it and handed it down to her. She gulped, closed her eyes for a moment with brows pulled in, and drained the cup.

"That's better." With care, as if the floor might play tricks, she transferred to the edge of an ordinary dining-chair. "May I have some of the dry biscuits and soft cheese . . . and more coffee, please."

He gave her a napkin and a laden plate, and heaped his own plate with slices of tinned tongue and vegetable salad. They ate without speaking, and presently she sighed and pushed away her empty cup.

"I must have been hungry, after all. That was good." She stared with swift concern at the brightened glow of the lamp, and turned her head towards the grass-matting screen at the window. "It's already dark. I must go."

"Don't be absurd. It's only six-thirty."

"Won't your friends be curious about the car?"

"They'll conclude that I'm being visited by a government official from the station. Would you like that cigarette now?"

She selected one and sat forward smoking it, an elbow on the table.

"Unreal, isn't it, our being together in your mud hut? I shall never believe that this really happened."

"You planned it," he said curtly.

"Not exactly. From Dakar down I heard Cape Ricos mentioned a few times, and I naturally decided that if the boat put in for long enough I'd try to see you. Had we sailed past I'd have posted the cheque to the lawyer who handled your affairs in Parsburg."

"What about being whole-minded before you settle with a husband in Port Cranston?" he sardonically reminded her.

"That was less important. I knew I was nearly over the . . . hurt you inflicted."

"What sort of chap is he?"

"Charming. A year or two younger than you, of good family and a highly respected citizen."

"Just your medicine, Teresa."

She ignored the satire. "I believe so, too. I've told him about . . . you."

"How nice. Doesn't he object to marrying a woman who isn't in love with him?"

"Apparently not," she answered coolly. "He proposed before I went to England, but I wasn't ready for it. I asked him for time to weigh up the matter."

"Is he aware that you're now on your way to his arms?"

She shook her head. "I shall telephone him from Cape Town. I'm not cheating him. He's been married before, for a short while."

"Very convenient — you'll start even with each other. What's his name?"

"Richard Barnwell. He's South African." Tess got rid of her cigarette. The smile she turned upon Dave in his easy chair was jaunty. "I'm often grateful that you were my first love, Dave. I ought to have expressed my gratitude to you for condescending to teach me how not to love."

"Forthright little cuss, aren't you?" he said pleasantly. "But I'm not rising to it, Teresa. Never again, my sweet one." He stretched his legs and waved a moth from his bare knee. "Take a more comfortable chair and tell me your impressions of the places you've visited."

She expanded upon her delights and disappointments of the last few months, but remained seated in the straight-backed chair near the table while she did so. Her smile was losing spontaneity, and a frown of strain began to appear above her eyes. Her tone, though, retained its casual inflection till she could find no more to say. Then she looked at her watch.

"It's getting towards eight."

"I know." He pushed himself to his feet by the chair arms. "Sure you don't want a wash before we go?"

"I'm grubby, but . . ." Her fingers clenched white over the edge of the table as she rose. She held her head lowered. "Do you keep some sort of antiseptic cream?"

"I knew there was something!" Firmly he took her chin and raised it. "You're in pain, aren't you?"

She jerked away. "You said the bathroom was through that door?"

"Your fool pride! What is it?"

Her smile was brittle and contorted. "A prickly heat rash, that's all."

"Round your waist?"

"Yes. It started four days ago, in Accra. It was getting better, but driving in the heat has made it sting. Dave . . . Dave, please don't!"

With gentle but determined hands he was removing her jacket. She heard his involuntary exclamation, felt his warm palm laid lightly over her back and his breath in her hair as he bent for a closer inspection. Gingerly he fingered a fold of the blouse and detached it from her skin. She made a small sound of agony and he let go and straightened.

Quietly he said: "Sore back is common when you drive for long in this climate, particularly if you're mad enough to wear no vest. Your rash has become a mass of broken blisters. It was brave of you to act jolly in the midst of stark pain — brave and senseless, and entirely typical. You're not sailing tomorrow, Tess."

"But I must! You promised to take me to the coast. I'll lie in the back of the car . . . cushions will help. I've got to go."

"Your Richard must wait," he said flatly. "I wouldn't subject anyone in such condition to several ours rumbling in a car. This mess must be given a chance to heal, or it will take infection."

"I can't stay in Lokola!"

"You'll have to. We'll find you somewhere to sleep for a couple of nights. There's another woman here — she'll probably put you up." Calmly, yet tight-mouthed, he looked down into her face. "Lousy luck for you, Tess, but you've no choice. Go along to the bathroom and I'll bring a dressing-gown and the medical kit."

Twenty minutes later they were in the living-room again. Tess, wrapped in a navy silk robe she had never seen before, was lying in the lounger among the white pillows from Dave's bed; her hair was tousled, her expression bleak and fatigued.

He stood back from making her comfortable. "Don't take it so hard. Once I've fixed you up with a place to live, you and I needn't meet till you're fit enough to make the ride to the coast."

"What will you tell them — the others here — about me?"

"The truth — with dilutions." At the scrape of a foot in the veranda he stiffened. "This will be Luke Walton. Stay where you are and leave everything to me."

The wire-mesh screen clanged open and finger-nails clicked against the panel of the door. Familiarly, the handle was turned and Luke lounged in.

"Say, Dave, there's a bit of a dam'-fool mystery. Langland has come up from the station . . ." He stopped abruptly, his thin tanned jaws a trifle slack. "I beg your pardon."

"Come in," said Dave easily. "Oh, so Langland's with you. What's the mystery?"

Langland was the education officer, a burly man of large appetites. His glance, as it became accustomed to the lamp-light, found Tess; it flashed to Dave and then went seeking again, almost stroking over the length of her weary body.

"There isn't one," he said softly. "Not now. Johns reported that someone had come here in a govern-ment car. The D.O. still has gun-running on his mind and he asked me to investigate.

Dave smiled. He saw Luke Walton, apparently winded, propped against the wall and staring with unwonted intensity at the pale silky hair and pure feminine features. He was also conscious of Langland's concentration of interest in the slim, supine body swathed in his dressing-gown.

"I was on the point of going down to Redding's. We can talk on the way."

"He's gone to Fort Leppa, and taken Mrs. Redding. She heard about the cases of sleeping sickness and got terrified."

"I see." Dave was standing in front of the lounger with his back to it. His thoughts moved fast and with precision. Avia's flight left Lokola womanless. Of the ten men in the district six were bachelors and sick to the soul with their state. "Well, Langland, you may reassure the D.O. The car was borrowed in Cape Ricos this morning, and I shall send a boy back with it at dawn."

"So the young lady is staying?" The small eyes in their puffy setting glimmered. "You might introduce me, Dave."

Dave half-turned. "Don't get up, Tess. You've heard me talk about Walt. Here he is in the flesh, though he's mostly bone. And this is Bill Langland, who looks like the skipper of a bug-boat, but he once filched a degree which entitles him to the pay of an education officer." With an offhand smile and watchful eyes, he announced, "My wife, gentlemen."

CHAPTER TWO

TESS spent most of the next two days and nights on the lounger in Dave's living-room. He fixed it up with bed linen and brought in a mosquito screen each evening. She did not see much of him. He breakfasted on the veranda and cleared off till four or five in the afternoon. When he came in he made polite enquiries as he passed through to take a shower, and he did not appear again till dinner was ready.

Over the meal he talked of his job and about Walt and Brig. When coffee had been disposed of and

arettes lighted he moved about, without haste, se-
ring the window-blind at the glassless aperture, shift-
g her bed to catch the maximum of air and generally
rranging things for the night.

"Need anything?"

"No, thanks."

"Right. Good night, Tess."

"Good night, Dave."

He went out and the key snicked in the lock. She
guessed that he passed the hours till midnight playing
cards with the others. He came in quietly, the back
way, and the rest of the night was silent.

Unused to inaction, Tess seldom fell into a deep
sleep. There were times when, half-waking, she re-
lived those frightful days after the lawyer had told
her that the orange farm was to be sold. For more
than a fortnight Richard had neglected his business
to be with her; wherever she turned he had been
there with wordless sympathy and suggestions for killing time and deadening pain.

Presently, Richard grew into more than the
stranger who had befriended and sustained her. His
sister had married and, with unusual warmth, had
invited Tess to occupy one of the bedrooms of the
big, rambling house. The arrangement had suited her
for a while — till Richard had asked her to marry
him. After that she had to get away.

In England she had rigidly banished both Dave and
Richard from her thoughts. Her brothers' friends,
intrigued by the phenomenon of an English girl who
knew nothing whatever about England, and willing
to be fascinated by her slim brownness and the silver-
gilt hair, had not disguised their interest. Tess had
grasped at the fun they offered and wondered whether
she could settle in England. But within weeks she
was restless again, and inevitably had come the visit
to the shipping office to book a ticket for stage one
of her return to Port Cranston.

It was at Dakar that she first heard mention of
Cape Ricos, and afterwards, each time the name was
brought into a conversation she had questioned the
speaker.

One man, a hardened rubber salesman, had answered her taut query: "Yes, it's true enough. They've had several cases of blackwater over the last few months, but I've heard that it's worse inland, beyond the swamps, in places like Mbana and Lokola."

Tess had had a series of chaotic nightmares. By the time Cape Ricos was reached she found herself hoping dully that Dave had died of blackwater; that way he would be removed from her life for ever, and she could go ahead and marry Richard.

At the port she had learned that the rumour had arisen from two cases, one close upon the other. She was told that that particular fever could never become epidemic because it was chiefly the malaria-ridden who contracted it.

Tess should have gone back to the boat then, and unemotionally awaited departure; she should have soaked the pitted skin at her waist with calamine and avoided perspiring at all costs. Being Tess, she forgot everything except that Lokola was only a hundred miles away, and the possibility that Dave had picked up some other fever. She had to know.

It seemed foolish now that she should have been anxious about him; she should have accepted the fact that wherever she made her home there would always be Dave at Lokola to plague her subconscious.

The third afternoon Luke Walton came in. He brought her some flowers from the Redding's garden.

"They won't mind," he said. "It's a grouse with Redding that his wife has no interest in his garden; he'll be glad to have his blooms appreciated."

Tess was sitting up in a chair, her back well-cushioned and her feet raised to a stool.

"It's kind of you to think of me. I don't suppose Dave owns a flower jar, but there'll be a jug or something. Call the boy, will you?"

The flowers were arranged on a small table, blood-red splashes against the white wall.

"Sit down and have some tea with me," she invited. "It'll be pleasant to have someone to talk to."

Luke lowered himself into a dining-chair. Smiling, his unspectacular features had a certain charm, and somehow, the sight of his long brown shoes had for

Tess a soothing, homely quality. She felt that she and Luke were bound to use the same language. She took a cigarette and tilted it to his match.

"How long have you been here?"

"In Lokola? About six years, but I've lived up and down the coast since I was twenty. I've had eighteen years of it."

"I don't suppose you can imagine yourself living anywhere else?"

"I've thought about it . . . particularly when Dave moved out a couple of years ago. I kidded him like the others did, but if he'd asked me I'd have gone with him."

Tess smoked for a minute. "Think you could have settled to orange farming?"

"I don't know." He tapped his cigarette into an ashtray. "Beats me why Dave didn't — with you around. Can't think why in hell he came back here."

"He'd had enough of civilization." She pushed aside a book to make room on the table for the teatray. "Dave's happier without women," she said. "I'm sorry I came."

"You might give it a month's trial," he suggested.

Unguardedly, she said, "I might — if I were wanted."

"Oh." He slackened his knees and leaned on them, towards her. "I dare say you know me better than I know you. Dave might have told you about us —"

"A little," she admitted.

"Well, you came to us out of the blue. Dave hadn't let on that he was married. I can guess some things about him, but I didn't guess that, though I did have a pretty good notion that something had happened while he was away."

Her fingers curled into her palms. "Why?"

He gently shook his head. "He wasn't the same."

Luke was remembering things: the occasional raw cynicism in Dave's letters from Zinto; the derisive glitter in his eyes across the card table when he had unbent enough to describe some of his experiences as an orange farmer; and his flat refusal to go to the coast for a week-end's binge. Seemingly he was off both oranges and women.

110

Tentatively, Tess broke in, "You didn't believe Dave would ever tie himself up, did you?"

"It wasn't that." Any man was likely to meet a woman he couldn't have without marriage, he thought, but that was a low reason for marrying. "You oughtn't to have let him go. He'll never forgive you for it."

Tess looked at him queerly. "Why did you say that?"

Luke shrugged. "You've found his tenderest spot . . . and his meanest. He used to say, 'I'll never marry, Walt. Women are too damned hard.' You see what I mean?"

Yes, Tess saw. Luke, quiet, speculative and friendly, constituted quite a menace.

"When does the next boat leave?" she asked.

"There's one south in nine days. I'm shipping some oil in her."

"Does she take passengers?"

"When necessary, but she only goes as far as Lobito Bay."

"That'll do." Tess sighed and smiled. "As soon as I can walk freely I'll come and watch you going about your business."

"Dave told us you had a heat rash. Devil, isn't it, but fortunately they soon fade with resting."

Companionably he went back over the minor ailments of his apprenticeship in the tropics; light fevers, enteritis, scorpion bite. All had happened within his first two years, since when he had increased his whisky intake and grown the Coaster's immunity to the commonest ills. He went on to give details of the various jobs he had done, and related the incident which had led to his becoming a "palm-oil gentleman."

Tess laughed with him, and looked up to see Dave in the doorway. Luke got up.

"Hi, Dave. Hope you don't mind finding me here."

"Not a bit." The grey gaze rested on the brilliant bouquet and passed on. "It's going to be another steamy night."

Tess pulled herself carefully to her feet and invited, "Stay and have chop with us, Luke."

Luke hesitated.

"Thanks, but another night. See you later, Dave?"

"Probably."

"Right. So long."

They heard his tuneless whistling as he dropped down to the track and sauntered back to his own house. Dave kicked off one boot and started on the other.

"Listen, Dave," she said firmly. "I shall be able to travel tomorrow, or the following day at the latest. You must take me to Cape Ricos, and I'll wait there for the boat."

He poured a drink. "I wish it were that easy. What d'you suppose they'd say about a man who'd dumped his wife in a flea-ridden port and left her there?"

"That story has served its purpose. Tell everyone the truth."

His lips thinned. "You may have no regard for your own reputation, but mine means quite a lot to me, even here. If you're concerned about the construction your Richard will place upon it, I can only remind you that you came here of your own accord."

"I didn't intend to stay overnight. You made me do that!"

"Because I wouldn't let you commit suicide? I've seen a man take infection through a cut finger and pass out within days. With your back in such a condition I had no alternative but to make you stay."

"No one forced you to stretch your chivalry to the limit!"

"I said you were my wife," he told her coldly, "so that you wouldn't be plagued by woman-starved government officials."

There was a silence while Dave finished his drink, and Tess despondently piled up the magazines.

"I've got no clothes but this thing," she said without spirit.

"The boy pressed it up and washed the blouse."

"But Luke said the next boat is nine days away."

"It can't be helped. If Avia were here she'd lend you some frocks."

"Avia?" Tess twisted to watch his dark face. "Who is she?"

"Mrs. Redding. A good-looker, too, to save you asking."

Tess let herself down among the pillows and turned her face against the cool linen. She heard Dave walk out, and the water being tipped into the bath. Then a door closed and sounds were muted.

Dave did not go out straight after dinner. For an hour he scanned the tin mine reports and pencilled notes for discussion with Brigham. He sat at the desk, as engrossed as if he were alone, while Tess lay alternately dozing and following the fortunes of the insects which flittered about the lamp.

It was nearly ten before he got up, lit a cigarette and put the customary enquiry.

"Need anything?"

Tess altered her reply. "Only a car filled with petrol — and no interference."

"Grateful wench, aren't you? Don't get the notion that I'm keeping you here because it's like heaven to have you around again. It isn't."

"I know. But, Dave . . ." Tess quelled a tremor. "If you go on hating me, nine days will be a lifetime. You never did really understand about . . . Martin. You can't realize how it is to have a man of his kind clinging as if you were the only solid thing in the universe. I wasn't remotely in love with him and you knew it — but you allowed yourself to be ruled by anger and violence." The set of his features was a warning, but she had to go on. "You came here to forget me, but it hasn't worked, or you wouldn't still loathe me. To forget each other we've got to come out into the open. I don't believe there's any love left between us, but we'll never be happy with anyone else unless we make the test, by becoming just . . . friends."

"Finished?" he queried politely. "May I give you some advice, Teresa? I once had to be present at an exhumation; the remains were grisly and they got a man hanged. We'll leave ours buried. Instead of lying there awake analysing the differences between a man and a woman, try dreaming ahead. Richard will make an excellent husband, and give you the three well-spaced children without which no merchant's home is complete. Good night."

Her answer was brief and vehement.

Nine days more of his relentless enmity? Not if she could avoid it!

CHAPTER THREE

LUKE'S was the fourth and last house in the clearing. Inside it was shabby but meticulously neat; typical, as were the polished, worn shoes, of his well-ordered and much-used mind. Luke disliked clutter, which, perhaps, was why he had never married. The trouble was, it seemed pretty well impossible to straighten out a woman's ideas; she had too many of them at once, and no discrimination.

Dave's wife seemed to be an exception; she was matey, like a boy, yet her bones were fine, her skin soft and honey-coloured. At first she had looked as if Dave could have snapped her in two, but Luke wouldn't mind betting that she was tough as leather . . . and that at times she could be as yielding.

It didn't surprise him to come upon Tess in his shed next morning. She appeared fit, though a shade ludicrous in a baggy shirt of Dave's and a pair of exceedingly roomy shorts lapped over and belted round her waist. She grinned at him.

"Look appalling, don't I?" she said cheerfully.

"You certainly do. Did Dave see you like that?"

"No. He'd flay me." She strolled about sniffing at kegs and sacks. "Don't you sicken of the smell of palm-oil? What do you trade for it?"

"Hardware and cloth, but chiefly cash. It's easier."

"You'd make a heap more money if you ran an emporium as a sideline."

"There's already a native store at the village. They sell Manchester cottons — if you're stuck for clothes."

"Do they?" she sounded uninterested. "Do you ship all your palm-oil, Luke?"

"Most of it."

"How do you get it to Cape Ricos?"

"By rail. It would be too chancy to send it round by road, even if I had a lorry."

She gazed out at the surrounding arbutus trees and

plantains, the tall ferns tangled with vine. "Where's the railway station?"

"There isn't one. The mines run a private line to Fort Leppa, seventy miles away, and I have a contract with them to take my stuff. They load at the terminus, just below the official houses."

"No passenger trains?"

Thoughtfully, Luke shook his head. "None. Why the interest?"

She shrugged. "Merely curiosity. I wondered how Mrs. Redding made the trip to Fort Leppa."

"There's a road of sorts, but it's dangerous. About half-way between Lokola and Fort Lappa is another mine, at Mbana. You may have read about the Mbana riots a couple of months ago."

"I believe I did. Shooting, wasn't there?"

"That's right. Someone's running guns and inciting the natives, and they're using that road."

From the open end of a canvas bag Tess scooped some millet and trickled it between her fingers. "You'd think they'd have more sense than to play cowboys in this heat, wouldn't you?" she said carelessly. "Can you lend me a hat, Luke?"

Tess went out, past her own door and past Redding's; straight down into the trees. Luke hoped she hadn't decided to go visiting in that get-up. Her unselfconsciousness was slightly unnerving. She didn't seem particularly unhappy. Maybe he'd been mistaken yesterday; possibly she hadn't quite got over the soreness of the rash. It didn't occur to Luke that Dave might have made love to her. Her brightness wasn't soft and spontaneous; it had an edge to it.

Just after eleven Tess came back up the track. She walked slowly and pensively, the hat tipped forward now to shade her eyes. She sure had stamina, thought Luke. He couldn't remember seeing a woman about the place before four in the afternoon, and then they mostly appeared beneath a parasol in floating garments and clouds of perfume.

He sauntered down to meet her.

"See anyone?"

"Only a couple of half-breeds in uniform. Who are they?"

"Portuguese. They work with the construction gangs, and police the railway." With faint mockery he added, "Pretty little town, isn't it?"

"Men will stand anything for money. Dave will end up in a tropical hospital spending his filthy riches on a cure."

"It's up to you," said Luke, in that gently ironical tone of his.

As she entered the living-room she was smiling, but without mirth. The hat was dropped into a chair and she poured some tepid water and gulped it down. The taste was dreadful; brackish and medicated. No wonder the men had to flavour it with alcohol. Everything here seemed to hide sudden death.

And what had the men, to make up for such horrors? The same few faces about them, a game of poker, perhaps a sensation of power in being lords over a few thousand Africans . . . and money. For her part they could have it.

In coming to Lokola she had capped every other mistake in her life. Though she was not really sorry she had come. Had she sailed on down to the Cape with Dave still dragging at her heart-strings she would never have known peace. She had to see him here, in Lokola, to be aware of the infinitesimal role she had played in his life.

Meanwhile she must steel herself to meet Dave this evening and take care that the boy, Zula, should suspect nothing. She chose a book from the miscellaneous collection on the shelves, and went on reading it, through lunch and after. At about three she had a bath and got into her green suit. The shorts and shirt were shoved out of sight under the lounger and, after a second's thought, Luke's hat joined them.

While the boy snoozed in his hut she inspected the food cupboard and selected some tins of orange juice and a packet of rye biscuits. These were tipped into a washed flour bag and thrust alongside the felt hat.

She sought scissors and took them to the mirror above the bookshelves. For a long moment she regarded her reflection. Mouth and blue eyes were tense with conquered pain, the jaw-line was inflexible. She raised a tress of the pale silky hair which curled down behind her ears and rolled under into her nape. Her hand went round to finger the scar it hid, and a sharp, agonized breath escaped her. This was one job she must leave till later.

Dave came in at half past four. He drank some tea and had his bath. It was nearly six when he returned to the living-room and began to tidy his desk.

"We'll have an early meal," he said over his shoulder. "Brig's coming in. He's been seedy after malaria, or you'd have met him before."

"Oh." Tess waited till her pulses were nearly normal again before asking, "Will he stay late?"

"Probably. It means keeping you out of bed. You feel up to it, don't you?"

"What do I have to do?"

"Put on a smile and take a couple of drinks," he said laconically. "Walt noticed you hadn't a wedding ring, but Brig won't."

"What did . . . Luke say?"

"Nothing. I saw him look at your hand and come to some conclusion. No doubt he decided you flung it at me when we parted. Walt reads novels."

Tess got the impression that he would have gone on annoying her if Brigham hadn't knocked and brought his bulk into the room.

After the meal the two men talked about tin production and wages, while Tess sat resting her head against the back of a chair, willing herself not to look at her watch.

Presently cards and coins were produced. Brigham shuffled.

"Like to play, Tess?" from Dave.

"No, thanks."

"What about Walt?" said Brigham.

"He's sure to be in soon."

They played, almost in silence. Tess remained in the chair, a feverish knocking just above her eyes and the heat of apprehension in her body. Luke lounged in and stood by the table, smiling across at her. Dave hooked over another chair.

"Deal you in this hand, Walt?"

"If you like." To Tess he said: "I expect you're tired. Don't stay up for us."

Dave paused in dealing. His face darkened. "Mind your own business, Walt."

Luke's stare of amazement was quickly veiled. "Sorry," he murmured.

Brig said easily, "You did say she hadn't been too grand, Dave, and it'll be fresher in the bedroom."

The hand was finished and Dave stood up. "We'll go to your place, Brig."

No one demurred. Brigham and Luke said good night to Tess and went outside. Dave pressed out his cigarette and, without looking her way, followed them. The key snapped audibly in the lock.

Fully five minutes passed before Tess stirred. It was just after nine, so she had plenty of time. Dave wouldn't be back before midnight. It wouldn't do to wait till he had returned and gone to bed. He was a light sleeper and kept a gun under his pillow, and she'd bet that it was his policy to cripple an intruder first and ask questions afterwards. She didn't fancy a bullet in her leg. So she lit a cigarette and began to undress.

It was hot. A sticky wind kept lifting the screen at the window, puffing in the moist, heady odour of the jungle. Tess felt it over her skin as she pulled on the shirt and pants and fastened the metal loop at the waist. Teeth clamped, she stood before the mirror and cut off the hair which covered her neck. She tried on Luke's hat, shook her head and hacked off another inch. That was more like it.

Cosmetics, money, her passport and her cheque-book were transferred from the white suède handbag to her pocket; Dave could sole his shoes with the bag if he wished. Her suit and blouse were folded and stuffed into the flour bag with her food.

And now the most difficult task of all. She sat at the desk, a sheet of paper in front of her and Dave's pen poised. Then she began to write swiftly.

By the time you read this, at about seven-thirty tomorrow morning, I shall be a good many miles from Lokola. I fixed up transport quite easily, and all you have to do is explain my disappearance to Luke Walton and Brigham. I suggest you tell them the facts. I apologize for shaking you up, but from now on you may settle back among the whisky bottles and damp rot without fear of further invasion from me.

Tess paused, scribbled a signature and threw down his pen. She drank some water and ranged round the room a couple of times. This damned, stifling house. She would rather wait in the darkness of the trees.

She turned down the lamp, saw it spurt and die, and blinked hard to accustom herself to the blackness. It was simple to roll up and secure the screen, to drop her bag of goods on to the beaten earth, and climb up and wriggle through. Perhaps she had better re-fasten the screen in case Dave or a boy took a final stroll round. That was it.

Tess grasped the twisted top of the bag, skirted the bank of rubbery weeds which divided the houses and, keeping to the black shadows of the trees, she started down the track.

At last she reached the cover of the main railway shed, and she sat down with her back against it, clasping her knees. The wet heat, combined with an undeniable weight of misery, made her drowsy. For an interminable time she gave herself up to intermittent dozing.

"*Menino!*"

It came in a voice that was thick and soft and urgent. Tess grabbed her bag.

"I'm here, *senhor.*"

The man came forward, a short, rotund figure in khaki drill slacks and an old blue shirt. His face, square and swarthy, glistened in the arc of his torch.

"You are the boy who want lift to Fort Leppa. Ha?"

She sprang up. "Yes, *senhor.* Is it arranged?"

"It is unfortunate, *menino.* The *telheiro* is locked up. They fear rain."

"*Telheiro?*"

"The shed, *menino.* One cannot borrow a car."

Tess gripped the bag tighter. "I see. Your . . . friend told you I promised money?"

"Yes, *senhorito,* but it would take *much* money."

At the mention of cash she had graduated from

119

"menino" to *"senhorito."* Firmly she demanded, "How much?"

"Hear first what I have planned. The car is impossible, but trucks are ready to leave, loaded with ore, and other goods. There is one which is covered . . . a *carreta*. You understand, *senhorito?"*

"A railway carriage?" she hazarded.

The torch wavered with his shrug. "Something like. It carry some goods, but you are not big. There is space for you."

"Isn't it fastened up?"

The briefest pause, before the slurred, guttural answer. "Yes, it has padlock and bars, but there is a way into it which I know. What do you say, *senhorito?"*

"You're sure there's no other way of travelling to Fort Leppa tonight?"

"Quite sure, *senhorito."*

The alternative, of course, was to crawl back to the bungalow and live through more days of Dave's remoteness and cruelty. She and Dave had nothing else to say to each other. Whatever had existed between them was as dead as last year's mountain roses. Dead so far as Dave was concerned.

She had had enough of that brand of wretchedness; there could be no going back. . . .

"How much?" she repeated.

"Five pounds."

"I've only English money."

"That will do."

Tess paid him. "Lead the way," she said.

"Graças, senhorito." The money was inserted into his shirt, the torch was snicked off. "It is not far."

She followed him round the sheds, over a loading platform and down again, beside the trucks lined up on the rails. They came to a large iron container coupled between two tarpaulin-covered trucks.

"This is it," he whispered. "Wait."

He dropped flat on to his back, took hold of something and pulled himself under the wagon. She heard the dull clank of iron, and the man reappeared and sat up.

"Do as I do," he instructed. "The opening is small, too small for a fully grown man, but you are thin."

Perhaps you graze a little bit, that is all. I see with the torch that only one side of the *carreta* is loaded. You sit the other side, my friend, and I will replace the iron trap-door."

"But how do I get out at Fort Leppa?"

"That is arranged with the driver. When he lets you out he will expect some more money."

She might have known. It served her right for dealing with scum.

"Sell me your flashlight," Tess demanded.

The exchange was made. She lay and pulled herself under the wagon, looked up into the interior through a hole about eighteen inches by twelve. Her bag was thrust into the aperture, then her arms, so that her elbows could take purchase. The metal edge scraped her sides and hips. Thank heaven for the voluminous shorts. She knelt inside the wagon, panting.

"You are all right?" from the Portuguese.

She replied with a doubtful, "Yes."

"Good. I will replace the seal. *Boas noites, senhorito!*"

The trap fitted back into its place, and Tess subsided into a sitting position, feeling like a lone sardine in an outsize tin.

In the quietude her tenseness eased. She moved back a little and noticed a round ventilator in the roof of the wagon, a circular pattern of sky through the metal wings of a fan, which would serve to remind her that she was not altogether cut off from the outside world. But it wouldn't do to flash a light while they were stationary.

She sat on, worn and hopeless, till, with clangour and screaming, the train began to jerk forward. No yelling, no whistle; merely a gathering speed over wet, protesting rails. Now, the fan in the roof was whirling, puffing down gusts of warm air.

Tess got out a handkerchief to wipe grime and sweat from her face and hands. She pressed on the flashlight and surveyed her surroundings. She was in an ordinary goods van, her only company a pile of flat wooden boxes which, she thought, were conveniently sized to slide through the trap-door. Leaning over, she read the words stencilled on each box, "Alluvial Holdings Ltd., Fort Leppa."

She caught her breath. Grimly funny that she should leave Lokola in Dave's wagon, with Dave's consignment to the head office of his firm in Fort Leppa.

For a goods train it was travelling fast. At this rate they would reach Fort Leppa by dawn. She would be able to hide somewhere and change her clothes, and later present herself at the station to buy a ticket for the coast. Not for Cape Ricos, though. Some other port would have to do. For Dave's sake, she must be careful. A woman travelling alone in West Africa was bound to draw comment.

For Dave's sake. With the distance widening between them, Tess allowed herself to think about him. His dark hair and tanned skin, the twist to his mouth; the hardness which had angled his features. He couldn't blame her for the change in him; it had happened inside himself. Now, she doubted whether he had ever loved her in the marrying sense. There might have been other women since Zinto.

But Tess knew, with heart-wrenching certainty, that she could never love anyone as she had loved Dave Paterson. Richard had been sincere, generous and tender; he had helped to bridge the frightful chasm between Dave and a sane way of life without Dave. Richard had implied that their experiences were parallel, and for that reason alone their marriage must succeed. In Port Cranston it had sounded plausible.

Tess sighed to herself. No; Richard was out. He had filled his purpose by providing solid and convincing evidence to her brothers that she would be happier in South Africa. He had also proved a fillip to her self-esteem in dealing with Dave. But she couldn't face him again. It would be best for them both if she kept clear of Port Cranston.

Where to, then? Tess lifted her shoulders. What did it matter?

Then, so suddenly that she was flung on the iron floor, the train jostled and shuddered to a halt. It sounded to Tess as if all hell were free. Rain hammered all round her, thunder cracked tremendously

122

right overhead, and through it all she heard staccato, but unintelligible, shouting.

Unmistakably came the clatter of a tool upon the floor of her wagon. Tess jumped up and backed into a corner. She saw the oblong seal removed and two leathery arms inserted. The hands searched, grasped one of the boxes and manoeuvred it down through the hole on to the track. Heart pounding, Tess witnessed the removal of box after box, and heard exclamations in Portuguese from other men outside. Train thieves, of course. But what in the world did they intend to do with the contents of Dave's boxes? The stuff still had to be processed before it would yield gold.

There came an English voice. "You have counted the boxes?"

"Yes, *senhor*. Eighteen."

"The note says twenty. Look again."

A dark curly head thrust up into the wagon, a white beam of light moved slowly round it, illumining the other two boxes . . . and a pair of slim ankles.

"*Por deus, senhor!* There is a boy in here."

"A boy? What the hell! Yank him out."

"A *white* boy, *senhor*."

"Have him out, damn you."

Much later, it occurred to Tess that she could have defied the command, and perhaps had an amusing time over the impotent struggle of the Portuguese to enter the wagon. At the moment, however, she was too scared to disobey and, in any case, the English voice was disarming. In fact, she was almost glad to surrender and scramble out into the storm. The rain beat down upon Luke's hat and ran in rivers over her shirt-clad shoulders. But it had the good fresh smell of freedom.

"What were you doing in there?"

The peremptory query issued from beneath an oilskin-covered topi. The man was of average height, but his build was obscured by a large cape.

An Englishman would not easily be deceived. Tess answered in low tones: "I don't mind being caught, sir. I can explain."

"You'll have to, but there isn't time now." The man turned. "Umberto! Give this boy a coat and take him to the house. I'll question him in the morning."

A sweat-smelling covering was dropped over Tess' back.

"This way, *menino.*"

Rain lashed through the trees, lightning zipped horizontally among the branches. Tess waded, calf-deep in red mud, beside the corpulent Umberto.

"Where are we going, *senhor?*"

"You hear the boss. We go to the house."

"Which house?"

"You are not to mind," he said sharply. "If you were not white we would kill you."

"So?" she said, with something of his accent. "You are brave, *senhor.*"

"And you, *menino,* have the impudence. How did you get into the wagon?"

"Someone hit me and put me there. I cannot remember."

"You come from Lokola?"

"Where," she blandly enquired, "is Lokola?"

He stumped on. "So you cannot remember. The boss will see about that in the morning."

They came upon the house unexpectedly. It was a small log dwelling among the trees, unlighted, except for a dim lamp high in the banana-thatched veranda; the sort of place one would have small chance of finding by daylight and no chance at all of locating in the darkness.

Umberto opened the door. "Come in," he said. "On a night like this I think we may have a light. Is that you, Maria?"

The woman entered, large and ponderous in an old white nightgown, her head tied in a cloth. Her colour was light and she spoke Portuguese, but she had the flattened nostrils and thick mouth of the Negro. She listened to the man's explanation, and turned to peer at Tess.

"You are hungry, young master?"

"No. Only thirsty and very wet."

"You shall have warm drink and a towel, and I will find some dry clothes."

"Don't make him too comfortable," warned the man.

The old woman showed yellowed teeth at Tess in a smile. "Umberto makes much noise, but he is kind. Give me your hat, young master."

Well, this was it. The lamp would choose this moment to burn with exceptional brightness. Tess whipped off her hat and shook back her hair. Nonchalantly, she threw off the rainproof and pretended to warm her hands at the glass lamp-shade. The glow lit up fine features and drenched curls, the shirt pasted flat to her body.

"A . . . girl," the woman muttered hoarsely. "Umberto . . . what have you done?"

He passed a thick shaky hand over his face. "I did not know. The boss did not know, either."

Maria was almost on her knees to Tess. "Umberto did not mean to harm the missus. He only do what he is told."

"I swear it, *senhora*," the man mumbled. "I would not hurt a white woman. Three months ago I am just a plate-layer, with the railway. Then the boss come. He give me this house so that he can use it. Sometimes he sleep here. Every month he give me money which I save, to go back to Nazaré, in Portugal, where I was born. I swear that is all, *senhora*."

"I believe you," said Tess. "Give me dry clothes and a mule, and show me the road to Fort Leppa, and you'll never hear of me again. You can tell your boss I ran away."

The old woman broke into voluble thanks, which Umberto silenced with a groan.

"Quiet, Maria! We are both mad. The girl cannot be allowed to leave this house. She knows about the guns."

The guns. With studious abstraction Tess wrung drops from her hair. Luke had mentioned gun-running, and so had the education officer on her first evening at Lokola. Dave hadn't said anything about it, though. Those boxes had borne the name of his company and were presumably intended for the headquarters at Fort Leppa. They had been padlocked within a special wagon which, however, had a concealed opening that several people knew about. Gun-running and Dave didn't mix, and whoever was at the back of the shady business had a good idea that they didn't. That was a possible reason why Dave's mine was used as a cover.

"If you don't want a pneumonia case on your hands you'd better let me dry off," she said.

Maria stumbled out of the room as if she were balancing the world on her shoulders.

Umberto let out an unsteady breath. "I do not understand, *senhora*. Women are spies in the civilized parts of the world, but in Africa, no! You are not a spy."

"You're right. I'm not. For my part you may run guns all the way from here to Cairo. I suppose this is somewhere near Mbana?"

"You know this district?"

"I read about the Mbana riots. The natives used guns then."

"*Senhora!*" Umberto straightened to his full five-foot-three. "The boss does not sell guns to natives."

"What does he do then?" she asked shrewdly. "Sell them to a Portuguese middleman?"

This must have been near the mark, for Umberto oozed a sudden and visible sweat.

"You will please say no more." He hurried to the door. "Maria! Stay with the *senhora* and do not sleep. If she gets away the boss will kill us both!"

He needn't have worried. Tess had no urge for further adventures tonight. She was tired and achey, and when she tried to think deeply her brain jibbed.

Maria brought a new shirt and slacks. "These will fit better than those you are wearing. I am sorry we have no nice new frock for a lady."

Tess rubbed down and put on the dry clothes. She wondered whom they had been bought for, and decided that Maria might have a youthful son somewhere. A brisk towelling converted her lank hair into a mass of rough curls, not much different from the way she used to wear it at Zinto. Lord, she was weary.

"Where do I sleep, Maria?"

The woman creaked to her feet. "Come with me."

She took up the lamp and went first, her large, felt slippers whispering over the rough boards. From the living-room extended a brief corridor, and in each wall was a door. Maria opened that on the right.

"This is the bedroom of the boss. You may lie on this bed and rest, missus."

Eyes closed, Tess rolled on to her side. Dave was asleep in Lokola. How she yearned to be there, under the same roof, whatever his mood; to waken in the morning and hear his movements as he breakfasted on the veranda; to be ready with a smile when he looked in and said "So long" before going off for the day. She made a small sound and twisted on to her back.

"Have peace," murmured Maria from her seat near the door. "It will soon be dawn."

Day broke stealthily, spreading a sulphureous vapour over the forest. The storm had passed on, leaving Lokola blanketed in a sultry, dripping mist which runnelled the walls and collected in pools on the verandas. The houses were nearly as bad inside.

Just after six Dave heard the boy at the paraffin stove. He put his head round the kitchen door.

"Got any coffee ready, Zula?"

"In one minute, master."

"Take some to the missus, and tell her we have to eat in that room this morning."

"Yas, master."

He stood aside to let the boy pass, and turned back to survey the tiny drab kitchen. This certainly was a hell of a shack. Two rooms, a bath cubicle so restricting that you chipped your elbows, and this little dungeon for cooking and storing food. The houses were a lot bigger and brighter down at the station, and there was always one empty. Only yesterday the district officer had mentioned the fact. But somehow, Dave wasn't attracted. Going sour, he thought, and no wonder.

The boy was back, holding the tray, the whites of his eyes very prominent.

"No missus in that room, master."

"Leave the coffee there. She's probably in the bathroom."

"Not in the bathroom. No blanket, no pillow on the bed."

Dave suddenly recalled that her pillow was in his room. He'd seen it on the chair when he came in last night, and concluded that she'd made do with cushions. He strode through to the living-room. The place looked lifeless and stale. The big metal ashtray in the centre of the table still held dead matches and butts from last night. The sheets and blanket, folded square and fitted into the seat of the wicker chair, retained a faint imprint of her weight. Upon the lounger lay the usual two cushions . . . and the white suède bag.

Then he saw the note lying open on his desk. As he read it a bitterness pulled at his lips. Sweet kid, Tess. She meant her exit to match her arrival in lunacy. Except that Tess wouldn't view her behaviour as crazy. She had looked after herself for so long that the journey from here to Cape Ricos presented merely an unpleasant obstacle which had to be cleared.

He went out into the mist and sprinted up to unlock the shed. The three cars were there, as well as the mine lorry. In any case, they'd have heard an engine running; even small noises carried and echoed in the jungle.

Back at the house he called the boy. "Go down to the station," he instructed him. "The masters may not be up yet, but talk to each of the houseboys. Ask if a car is missing. Make certain, and be quick."

Now, there was nothing for it but to go to Walt. Dave shoved a cigarette between tight lips and walked up to the last bungalow. Luke came out in shorts and nothing else, wiping a smear of lather from his nostrils.

"Hello, Dave. Filthy morning."

"Walt, I want you to do something for me. I can't go to the workings today. They know what they're expected to do, and there's a couple of native foremen in charge, but if you'd just stroll around once during the morning and again after lunch they'll keep going."

"Sure I will." Luke grinned. "You've chosen rum weather for a day out."

"I'm going to Cape Ricos."

"So Tess got her own way after all?"

"What do you mean?"

Luke pushed his brow into pleats. "No offence," he said soothingly. "I'm not inviting you down my throat again."

"You'd better tell me what you know."

"I don't know anything, except that yesterday she was curious about means of transport from Lokola."

"What did she say?"

"I don't much care for your tone." Luke sounded injured. "If you think I've been getting fresh with your wife, go and ask her."

Dave paused, and with a vicious flick of the wrist disposed of his cigarette. "She's gone," he said. "Cleared out as if all she had to do was catch a bus."

Luke went grave. "Some girl, isn't she?" he remarked slowly. "When was it?"

"Must have been while we were card-playing. Couldn't have been during the night. I hardly slept."

"Oh." Luke forbore to put an obvious enquiry. "Didn't she leave any explanation?"

"Nothing helpful. She hadn't met anyone at the station except Bill Langland, and he hasn't the guts to risk a row."

"You believe she just hooked a car and slid away on her own?"

"I don't know what to think," said Dave savagely. "She's capable of going off on a donkey."

"To Fort Leppa?"

"No, to Cape Ricos. She's been over that road once."

"It's some track in a storm. Parts of it will still be under water."

"Don't I know it!" he said through his teeth. "As soon as the boy gets back I'm leaving, and if she's still alive when I catch up with her, I'll twist her neck."

"Sounds a bit drastic," Luke observed reasonably. "You ought to make allowance for her being high-spirited . . . and miserable."

Dave looked at him sharply. His mouth moved, as if to speak, then closed firmly. He dropped down to the path.

"Sure there's nothing else you'd like me to do?" Luke asked over the veranda rail.

Dave shook his head and disappeared into the mist.

Ruminatively, Luke pulled on singlet and shirt. Dave should never have married — or he should have chosen someone placid and hero-worshipping, and gone on raising citrus. If he did meet up with Tess there'd be a first-class slanging match and they'd part again. Dave didn't realize how much the girl thought of him, and probably wouldn't care if he did.

He was brushing his hair when Dave klaxoned. He came to the door.

"Whose car did she take?"

"No one's," said Dave curtly through the car window. "They're all there. She may not have left the district yet, but there's a chance that she's on the Cape Ricos road, in a hell of a fix. Walt," his tone dropped, "don't spill anything, but if you get any news, follow it up, will you?"

Luke gave the assurance and the car sped away.

One way and another, Luke had no appetite for lunch. The sight of his boy in faded shorts and grubby rag of a shirt emphasized the melancholy in his mind, reminding him of the depths of carelessness to which he was sinking. He had a whisky-and-soda, and was about to lie down when a car came up the track.

Hurriedly, he re-fastened his belt and went out. But it wasn't Dave. The vehicle was the usual black saloon used by government officials, and it stopped outside Dave's bungalow. The man who got out of it was Claud Kent, the district officer. Luke hailed him and went down to meet him.

"Good afternoon, Walton. Is Dave Paterson about?"

One thing about Kent, Luke told himself with wry admiration — he could always be relied on to be first a gentleman. He was a good D.O., but always first a gentleman.

"He's had to go out for a few hours. As far as I could make out it was some grievance down at the native camp the other side of the workings," he lied easily.

"I see. This matter is urgent. Any idea when he'll be back?"

"Not before dark, I should say."

"That's a nuisance. I was hoping to arrange . . ." He stopped. "Do me a favour, Walton. Send a messenger to contact Dave — give the boy a note saying that I'm anxious for an immediate discussion. He'll understand."

"I will."

Luke answered morosely and went indoors. He dozed in the afternoon quiet. When he got up again the gold-dusted sun, having at last dispersed the intervening moisture, was sliding exhaustedly down behind the cottonwoods. Everything was still wringing wet to the touch, but a vitalizing breeze stirred the plantains, and the sky was assuming the normal evening tinges of purple and flame.

A white-suited boy brought a note from the D.O. Had Walton anything to report? It was imperative that Dave be impressed with the importance of this matter as soon as he turned up. Keep your pants on, thought Luke wearily. But he scribbled a brief, optimistic reply.

It was after eight when he caught the sound of Dave's car. He could tell it was Dave by the speed. He slipped round the back of Brigham's house, climbed on to Dave's veranda and opened the door. The lamp was burning and the table laid for two. Luke had no time to wonder. Dave was just behind him.

Luke swung round and stared. "Dave —"

"You've heard nothing?"

"Not a thing. And neither have you . . ." He tailed off. Then, "I'll pour you a drink."

"Only lime and soda. I haven't eaten."

He looked it, too. His face was grim and sweat-streaked, his shirt, breeches and riding-boots caked with red mud. His eyes, bloodshot with the strain of long hours at the wheel on treacherous roads, rested, for a moment, on the wilted jungle flowers with which Tess had replaced Luke's offering from the Reddings' garden.

"She didn't go to Cape Ricos," he said. "The whole road through the swamp is several feet under water. Just in case she'd got through before it had risen too high, I followed the trail right round the swamp — it took three hours each way — but farther on there

131

was a landslide — the road had fallen right away. Natives told me it happened early yesterday and worsened in the storm. We're completely cut off from the port."

"That leaves Fort Leppa. Look, Dave. Have a wash and some food. You can't do anything more tonight."

"The Fort Leppa road will be in equally bad condition — though she had time to be well on the way before the storm broke. God knows how she travelled."

"What are you going to do?"

"I came back for petrol. I'm going on to Fort Leppa."

"It's no good in the dark. Wait till the morning."

Dave called the boy. "Zula!"

"I'll go with you," Luke said, "but for Pete's sake go down and see Kent first. He's been up here for you, and sent a boy, too."

"What's it about?"

"He used all the adjectives meaning urgent and said you'd understand."

Dave paused. "Oh . . . I'd forgotten that. I haven't time to do anything about it now." To the waiting boy he said, "Get me some cold chop and a flask of coffee."

"You'll have to see him, Dave. If you do get to Fort Leppa tonight, you won't be able to trace Tess till daylight."

Dave took a deep, angry breath. "I suppose you're right. She'll be snug in a club bedroom."

He had a quick wash, swallowed some hard biscuit with meat and a drink. Luke went out to get the car filled.

Ten minutes later Dave presented himself at the white house of the district officer. With an anxious smile Claud Kent invited him in and closed the lounge door. His nod indicated the stained breeches and shirt.

"Good of you to come right away, Dave, but I'm afraid it's got too late to do anything tonight. Have a drink?"

"No, thanks. Did something happen to our rig-up last night?"

"Plenty. The note advising the despatch of the

132

twenty boxes reached our objective — whoever he may be. The goods train was held up and the boxes removed. Your plan was a good one, Dave, but the storm spoiled it for us. Every trace of the hold-up has been washed away."

"That's bad," said Dave mechanically.

"It's worse than bad. As soon as those boxes are opened and found to contain rock chippings the gang will know we're on to their methods."

"We were aware of that yesterday. If the police had co-operated and hidden in one of the trucks, as I suggested, it might have got results."

Kent shrugged. "There are not enough of the police, and they happen to be following their own line of investigation. All I could do was instal a watcher. McLaren did it — very ably, considering he had to stay under cover, but all he could tell us about the position was that the train stopped this side of Mbana. He thought the boxes were loaded into a car."

"He thought!" said Dave contemptuously. "The whole set-up was ruined because McLaren hadn't the nerve to get out and pile up a few stones to mark the spot."

"That's hardly fair. The man was told to carry on to Fort Leppa and report immediately."

Dave stood up. "We went through all the elaborate business with natives and Portuguese, had the wagon carved open and the stencilled boxes planted. It took us three days, and McLaren ruined the whole show in five minutes."

"McLaren did as he was told," Kent reiterated. "At Fort Leppa he had the wagon opened properly at the side, and examined it."

"What did he find . . . peanut shells?"

"As a matter of fact he did find something." The district officer unlocked a deep drawer of his desk and lifted out a small, limp white sack, which he placed on the table in front of Dave. "Take a look in there."

Dave did. After a second his hand went in to bring out a tin of orange juice, and then another, a packet of rye biscuits . . . and a roll of green linen from which dangled a dejected cascade of white ruffles.

His voice, when he spoke, was oddly harsh. "Is your assistant busy just now, Claud?"

"Not feverishly. Why?"

"Will you give him instructions to keep an eye on the workings for the next day or two?"

"Of course, but where will you be?"

"Somewhere between here and Mbana," Dave answered quietly.

CHAPTER FOUR

UMBERTO was singing in a voice which had once been clear and pulsing. Years and the humid heat of the tropics had roughened his throat and made him nasal, but the lyric poured with amazing sweetness from his unprepossessing mouth.

As the song ended he slapped the table. "You have it, *senhora*. Not a wrong note that time. You play very good."

"Thanks." Tess twanged a chord and laid the guitar on a chair. "You must teach me another one with a little less love and more fire."

"Maybe tomorrow."

Tomorrow. Tess pressed back her shoulders. Another day of it? Living in this house in the forest was like being walled up in a tomb. This was her second day and she had seen no one but Umberto and Maria, eaten nothing but a little of the macaroni and rice which seemed to be their main diet. They were kind, but too frightened to let her stray from the clearing. She was not even permitted to take a dip in the tin tub without Maria as spectator, though Umberto was very careful to accord her all the privileges due to a lady.

Maria came in and spread a square of Kaffir weave over the table. In her bright headcloth, her long, full skirt drawn in at the waist and the washed-out cotton blouse pulled up with a tape at the neck so that her big ageing breasts swung within its voluminous folds, she had the appearance of a swarthy peasant. But Tess had found that at heart she was more African than Portuguese.

The bowl of rice appeared, supplemented tonight by a mound of shredded raw onion which reeked through the room in a pungent blast. Maria brought a crazed willow-pattern plate, and a knife and fork.

"You eat now, missus."

"Take away the onion, Maria."

The woman frowned anxiously. "Onion is good. White missus cannot eat so much rice."

"I know. Take that, too. Just coffee, Maria."

"If you do not eat you will be sick."

Not so sick as if I do eat, Tess thought. Umberto looked sad. He gathered up the dish of onions and bore it away to the back room where he and Maria ate and slept. Maria gazed sorrowfully at the rice.

"Perhaps with more salt?" she suggested.

"Just coffee," Tess repeated.

"But, missus . . ."

At that instant the woman shrank back, and Tess twisted round to see the cause. A man had entered the room by the main door and was securing the latch after him. An ordinary-looking, middle-aged man, in the usual khaki drill outfit covered by a raincoat. He came forward into the light, revealing a pleasant, ruddy face, with a small greying moustache and dark, white-flecked hair.

"Good evening," he said. "All right, Maria. Leave me alone with the lady." He threw his coat over the back of a chair and looked at Tess. "Sit down again. You and I must have a talk."

She sank back into her chair at the table, and he sat across from her, lighting a cigarette.

"The other night you thought I was a boy," she managed.

"I remained under that impression till this afternoon, when Umberto got word through to me. I would have come before, but there have been washaways on the road. Tell me your name."

"Isn't it usual for the gentleman to be presented first?"

"Not in a case like this. You're in a very unfortunate position, young woman. In fact, I'm very worried about you."

"I'm beginning to get worried about myself," she

135

said. "I hadn't any intention of being mixed up with gun-runners."

The pause was almost imperceptible. "I'm afraid I must insist on knowing your name and where you came from."

"If I did give you a name it might easily be a lie."

"But, my dear young lady," he leaned towards her, genuinely concerned, "you must have a relative of some sort in the province. A woman in these places either has a husband, a father or a brother who is responsible for her safety."

"I'm the exception, which is rather lucky for you, isn't it?"

"Where did you board the train?"

"What does it matter? I've told you I have no connections of any kind in this country, but you daren't release me in case I split on you. We're at something of a deadlock, aren't we?"

He lay back, regarding her curiously. "The more I learn about women, the more they astonish me. Aren't you frightened at being caught up in this tangle?"

"I was, the first night. Since then I've existed on rice and macaroni, which seem to have a narcotic effect on the emotions. Also, I'm so completely in your power that it's not much use being frightened. You know," she pushed back on two legs of her chair with more sangfroid than she felt, "you haven't at all the villainous cast. I'd have taken you for anything but a gun-runner."

The man half-closed his eyes as if to ward off cigarette smoke. His voice hardened.

"I'm not a gun-runner. I do a legitimate trade with the Portuguese."

"But you'd rather no one knew about it."

"That's my business." He turned his head towards the back of the house. "Umberto!"

The Portuguese must have been hovering close, for the door shot open at once and he appeared.

"*Senhor?*"

"This lady was searched when she arrived?"

"Not searched, *senhor*. Maria gave her fresh clothes — those she is wearing now. In the pockets of the old

136

ones I found a powder-box, some English money and a cheque-book."

Tess felt the comforting corners of her passport against her side and smiled.

"Bring them here," said the "boss".

He examined the things carefully, leafing through each of the stubs in the cheque-book. To the last he gave close attention.

"Who is Dave?" he demanded.

Tess came back on to the four legs of her chair with a bump. Could she have been so damned silly. . . .

"A friend of mine," she said quickly.

"In this district?"

"No."

"This is for a very large amount and dated only six days ago."

"What of it? I posted it to the Cape."

"Where were you then?"

"At the coast — Cape Ricos."

"Why did you come inland?"

"I've been asking myself that for several days."

The man got into his coat. "Stay on guard, Umberto," he said. "I'll come back later."

"To sleep, *senhor?*"

"I don't know."

Without another glance at Tess he hastened to the door and let himself out.

Casually, she reached over, picked up her belongings and stuffed them into her pockets. Umberto despondently shook his head.

"The boss is displeased," he said. "It is a pity. He is a good boss."

Tess was too angry with herself to pay further attention to Umberto. Had the man guessed who "Dave" was? And what could he do if he had? If only there were some means of escape from this prison, some way of evading those two pairs of keen eyes for just long enough to secrete herself in the undergrowth. But it was practically hopeless. These two were scared of the man, or rather scared about the part he had forced them to play. She doubted whether Umberto knew the "boss's" name or where he lived. Possibly the man was a stranger, a visitor to the district for the express purpose of making illicit money. When the chiefs ran out of cash he would go, leaving only a native nickname behind him.

Umberto sat glumly watching her, but when Maria came in he got up and walked out.

Tess said, "I'm going to bed, Maria."

"That room belong to master. He come back."

"I don't care. I feel like death."

With bowed head Maria followed her. Last night Tess had undressed. Tonight she hadn't the energy to do more than collapse upon the blanket and let Maria pull off her shoes. There was no lamp, but she sensed that the half-breed had gone over to sit in her usual chair, her eyes wide open. Soon, Tess slipped into an uneasy sleep.

Some time later she was awakened by voices. Maria must have opened the door, for as soon as Tess was thoroughly awake they came quite clearly, the tones of the "boss" and those of an English woman.

"You can't do that sort of thing with a girl," the man was protesting. "Her presence in the wagon was entirely accidental and she's suffered a great deal already. Umberto tells me she can't take their food, and is practically starving."

"If so, her condition is just right for what I suggest." The words dropped like sharp little stones. "You say she can have no idea where she is, that she must be weak from lack of food. You have a tender heart, haven't you, darling? Don't let it blind you to the wretched spot we're in. Those faked boxes mean that it's time to get out or make ourselves inconspicuous — and I'm not ready to get out. This house must be destroyed, the Portuguese and his wife sent away. The girl is a danger —"

"I can't do it."

"Darling, for both our sakes."

The man's voice fell to a caressing murmur.

Abruptly, the voices were cut off. Tess turned on the bed to face the door and saw that it had been closed, smelled the spicy, native smell of Maria. She had been listening, too.

"Maria," she whispered.

"Quiet, missus." Trembling with terror, the woman came near. "They will not harm you."

"I'm not so sure. If you're set free go to the police."

"They would take Umberto to prison."

"Not if it led to the capture of these people. Is she his wife?"

"I do not know. Always before he has come alone." With sudden urgency she smote her hands together. "Talk no more."

She was back in her chair just in time. There came a tap at the door and it was thrust open.

"Maria, tell the lady to get up and bring her into the living-room."

"Yas, master."

Tess took her time. She came blinking into the light and grasped the back of a chair. The man was alone, standing on the other side of the table. His expression was set, his glance chilly and withdrawn. He bent and pushed towards Tess a cup of coffee.

"I can't face any more of that tonight," she said.

"Drink it!"

"I don't want it."

"You're going a journey. I insist!"

Tess tried to stiffen her knees. She gulped at the coffee; it tasted even more horrible than usual. Umberto, his gaze lowered, brought in an old loose coat. Apparently upon instructions, he cut out the maker's tab and went through the pockets. The "boss" ordered Tess to put it on. Then he turned down the lamp and opened the main door.

"I shall be about an hour, Umberto. Have your things packed when I return."

Tess was out in the darkness, a firm hand on her arm.

"This way."

The courtesy with which he seated her in the car would have struck Tess as comical had she felt anything like normal. But her whole being had a floating sensation and it was an effort to keep her eyelids apart. As they started off behind dimmed sidelights, she was overcome by a wave of physical sickness which gradually passed off and left her shivering and exhausted. This was no revulsion from hunger.

"I hate having to do this," her companion said jerkily, "and nothing would have persuaded me to it, if I hadn't seen that counterfoil in your cheque-book. I can't risk your contacting Dave Paterson."

"You . . . you needn't worry. I was . . . running away from him."

The car slowed. "Why didn't you say so before! I'd have got you on to a boat."

"It isn't . . . too late."

"I'm afraid it is," he said, and stepped hard on the accelerator.

CHAPTER FIVE

LUKE took a swig of brandy from his pocket flask. Spots, which were not altogether attributable to the blistering mid-day heat, danced before his vision. His liver was turning on him, and why shouldn't it? Patrolling the baked, rutted trails for a stretch of forty hours with scarcely a five minutes' doze, eating cold beans and stale bread, and listening continually for Dave's signal . . . it was enough to upset any man's balance.

He wouldn't have minded if there were any hope of finding Tess, but she'd been gone nearly three days and one could cover quite a few miles in that time, even in West Africa. The fact that she was not to be traced in Fort Leppa didn't prove much. Luke couldn't understand Dave's fanatical combing of these fifty square miles of forest. Gun-runners don't hang around once they're tumbled to, nor do they leave evidence of kidnapping all over the place. He wouldn't mind betting that by now Tess had got round by rail to the port, and was calmly, if rather unhappily, awaiting her boat. Pity she couldn't get a laugh out of the spectacle of Dave bumping along native footpaths on a government motor cycle, searching for her.

The double pistol shot had echoed before he grasped what it was. In a reflex action he pressed the starter and swerved out to the centre of the track, his ears straining above the racket of the engine. The signal came again, from not so very far away, to the right.

Steady now, Luke told himself. It was probably just some thread of conjecture which Dave wanted him to follow up — like the footprints yesterday which had obligingly led him into a mass of hellish thorn and stopped dead. He braked and waited. Good, that was the cycle horn. He honked back and slid out onto the grass.

Within a couple of minutes he had joined another path which ran parallel to the road, and round a bend he came upon the motor bike.

"Here, Walt!"

Luke turned, and nearly froze. Dave was crouching among vines and jungleweed. Raised across his knees, her face white and still against his shirt, lay Tess. Luke muttered something and dropped beside him, saw the terrible mask of Dave's face and automatically looked away and laid the back of his hand along her cheek.

"There's a faint warmth. What do we do, Dave?"

"Take her to Fort Leppa."

"Aren't you going to try to revive her here?"

"I did. She remained unconscious — but retched. Her mouth smells bitter. She's been given . . . poison."

Neither spoke after that. Dave lifted her. Luke threw the old coat in which she had been wrapped over the motor cycle, and hurried ahead to spread the car rug along the back seat.

The journey took an hour, but Luke did not look round or speak over his shoulder till they had entered the walled town of white buildings, Mohammedan mosque and narrow, tortuous streets.

Then, "The clinic or Doctor Greaves?" he asked.

"Greaves — he'll be discreet. We don't want it all over town."

Dave said: "Go and tell the doctor. I'll carry her in."

There was no hitch. Dr. Greaves got up from his lunch and made a cursory examination while he shot questions. After which he nodded.

"You'd better go for a walk, Paterson — or better still, go and eat a good lunch at the club. Come back in a couple of hours."

"You may need help."

"If I do, my wife is here."

Dave came out to the porch, where Luke waited. "Let's get a drink."

"All right. What did he say?"

"Not much. As soon as you've had a bite you'll have to go back and see the D.O. Tell him everything, and make him realize that for the time being he must keep away the police."

"But they ought to be brought in!"

"Not yet." Dave paused, his eyes narrowed and glittering. "She's not going through the formal police third degree till she can stand it — and by that time I may have done their work for them. But I shan't use poison."

Luke did not comment. He drove down to the club, made a lightning meal of some salad, and stated that he was ready to return to Lokola.

"Don't forget," Dave said. "We keep it quiet — between you, Claud Kent and me. If he goes all official, remind him that should it become known that she's still alive she'll be in further danger."

It was nearly six o'clock before Dave was allowed to enter the small room where Tess lay. She was wearing a pink nightdress belonging to Mrs. Greaves, and the mosquito net was drawn round the bed, but only half-way up the side next to the small table. She had slept for an hour or two and then been wakened to take a little thin soup and fruit pulp. The doctor was still out, but Mrs. Greaves showed Dave into the room and left him there.

He drew up a chair and sat down, scanning her thin face and the dull eyes. He spoke softly.

"How do you feel now?"

"Fairly well," she said lifelessly.

"Did you get some food down?"

"Yes."

"That means the worst is over. You'll soon be strong again."

"I hope so."

"Tess," his tone was gentle and deliberately steady, "can you answer a few questions?"

"I'll try."

"Tell me the last thing you remember before being brought round by Dr. Greaves."

The pale lips parted, but it was a moment or so before she could speak. "He . . . the man —"

"Any idea who he was?"

"No. They called him the 'boss'."

"Go on, Tess."

"He made me drink some coffee. We were in a car and I believe I . . . passed out. Then we came into the air again . . . he must almost have carried me. He . . . he kept saying, 'I'm sorry, I'm sorry'. Then I was alone, clinging to a tree."

"Take your time." He covered the hand lying near him on the blanket with his own. "Does talking about it distress you?"

Her tongue stole out to moisten her lips. "No."

"But you must have been frightened."

"The nausea came again, much worse. That frightened me. Then I was sick — dreadfully, though I hadn't eaten all day — and a ghastly taste came into my mouth. I walked a little way, and collapsed."

A muscle tautened in his jaw. "The sickness saved you. Don't say any more, unless you want to."

For several minutes she lay perfectly still, with her eyes closed. Dave slipped her passport from the table into his pocket.

"Strange that . . . you should be the one to find me," she said at last.

"Not strange at all. I've searched continuously since Thursday morning."

"You must be very tired."

He bent closer and spoke urgently. "I've weighed up a lot of what happened to you, Tess. There was a shack of some kind among the trees. You'd be there still if they hadn't discovered that the boxes were faked and planted. After that they had to get rid of you and obliterate traces. Presently, when you feel able, I'd like you to describe the man to me."

The room was darkening, but he did not light the lamp. He could feel the pulse at her wrist, weak but regular; and there was a slight dew each side of her forehead. For the first time she looked at him.

"Those people . . . don't go after them, Dave. Let

143

the police do it. After all, I asked for it. I ought to have had the pluck to . . . to stay it out at Lokola."

"One person doesn't have every kind of courage. I was lousy to you — and my only excuse is that I felt lousy myself. I'd spread a sort of film over the past and you came along and ripped it away. I couldn't look at you without remembering what we'd been to each other."

She was silent again. When next she spoke it was to explain how the "boss" had looked and talked. She told him a little about Umberto and his wife, and made wry reference to the pasty and well-salted macaroni and rice which had undoubtedly saved her life.

With a ghost of a smile she said: "Try a couple of days on that diet, Dave. I guarantee you'll starve on the second."

His hand moved up to her elbow and gripped. "You certainly know how to take it," he said.

Her fingers turned and caught his sleeve. "You must learn how to take it, too. I'll do whatever you wish — lie low here or go somewhere else — but only if you'll promise to let the police handle that gang."

"Don't worry. I'm not after the gang."

He bent his head and kissed her fingers, leaned over to set his mouth to her forehead.

"Dave . . . hold me," she pleaded below her breath.

He slid first one arm under her and then the other. She quivered for a second as his cheek touched hers, and then he felt her tears. His arms tightened.

"You'll have to stay in Fort Leppa for the present," he whispered close to her ear. "I'll arrange for Mrs. Greaves to buy you some clothes, and she'll look after you till you're on your feet again. Don't go beyond the garden. Just concentrate on being well and happy."

"What about you?"

"I'll spend the night somewhere around, but I shall leave too early tomorrow to see you."

"You're returning to Lokola," she said in flat, dry tones.

"I've done no work since Wednesday. Besides, I have to allay curiosity."

"Yes, that's rather important. The preposterous fiction had slipped my mind."

"Don't, Tess." He let her lie back again, and straightened the sheet. "Shall I go now?"

"Yes."

He kissed her cool, unresponsive lips. "I'll be back within a few days. Don't take any chances."

In the hall he met the doctor.

Bluntly, he asked. "You're sure there'll be no complications?"

"As sure as a doctor can be. Her vitality is naturally low after such an experience. It's merely a matter of rest and correct feeding."

"In that case I'll go to Lokola tonight."

"I'd advise you to take a few hours' sleep before travelling."

"I'll rest better if I can clear up a few points first. Thanks for all you've done, Doc. Good night."

Dave pondered. He could borrow a car easily enough at the club. Redding was staying there, and he knew one or two other residents. But he would sooner leave the town unobtrusively. He approached a bearded, white-turbanned Hausa, and gave him a ceremonial greeting. Did this most worthy son of a noble family know of anyone who owned a car and would be willing to hire it out for one week?

A Hausa will trade anything, even that which has no positive existence. Dave got his car, and by seven-thirty he had left Fort Leppa well behind him.

The days were long and dreamy, the heat within the walled town so intense that few white people used the streets during the day. Tess had drifted into a state of mind in which nothing had much importance. She read novels or merely sat in the veranda and drowsed. Mrs. Greaves was usually busy over her husband's clerical work, or out attending various committees for the welfare of the natives. The doctor himself came home only for meals. So most of the day Tess was alone, except for the houseboy who meticulously followed his master's instructions in regularly bringing her meals. She seldom thought about the town, with its sixty white inhabitants and continual, if slender, flow of visitors from small stations like Lokola.

Thursday evening came before she had a visitor. Dinner was over and the Greaveses had gone to a friend's house for bridge. A party was in progress at the house across the road. Tess couldn't see anything because the place was screened off by casuarinas, but the music and laughter came over clearly, and made her restless. Not that she had any desire to dance or sing, or even for company. It was merely an atmosphere that shut her out, made her too conscious of her own isolation.

When Luke came up the drive she nearly cried aloud, "Thank God!"

He came on to the veranda and stared down at her with an odd, crooked smile.

"You look wonderful," he said.

"I don't feel it."

"I mean, you look wonderful to me, after last Saturday. How's everything?" He dropped into a chair.

"Progressing. In fact, I'm ready to leave this house."

"You mustn't do that," he said quickly.

"Dave's orders?" she queried. Then, point-blank, "Isn't he coming?"

"Of course he is . . . later tonight. You may not see him till morning, but he's staying the week-end."

"That will be nice."

She had spoken non-committally, but Luke's expression went keen.

"If, instead of boarding a freight train, you'd come to me, I'd have helped you."

"I know, but I couldn't cause trouble between you. It's no good now. Dave has my passport."

"You still intend to leave him?"

She drew a shaky breath. "Luke, take me for a walk. I'll put a scarf over my head and even wear a veil if you insist, but for heaven's sake take me for a walk!"

Conquered by the undisguised anguish in her voice, he muttered: "Well . . . perhaps to the end of the road. But make it a big scarf. That gilt curly cut of yours can be seen a mile off."

At the gate she said: "No car? Where did you leave it?"

"Outside the club. I walked up."

They strolled between well-treed gardens and

brightly-lit houses to an expanse of thorn scrub that smelled of the balsams and sage which clung here and there to a crevice in the stone outcrops. On the way back they threaded the avenues to prolong the distance. Except for an occasional car there was no one about and, with her arm caught comfortably close to Luke's side, Tess lost a little of the hunted feeling. But when, at a turning, she exerted a slight persuasive pressure, he demurred.

"Not down there, Tess. That's the centre of the town."

"Nobody knows me here."

"We hope not. You've had enough exercise, anyway."

"That's not much farther."

"We're near enough. This is the back of the club."

"Quite a number of cars —" She stopped abruptly.

One of the cars was detaching itself from the queue; a large one with the interior softly-illuminated. Dave was driving it, smiling as he curved out and put on speed. At his side sat a woman whose sleek, dark head was turned his way. In the moment of passing her profile was clear-cut and beautiful.

Tess relaxed her grasp of Luke's arm, and her feet began to move again.

"So you came in Dave's car," she said without expression. "That was why you walked to the house."

"I wasn't trying to fool you. We went to the club to book rooms."

"And Dave asked you to come and see me while he — Luke, who is that woman?"

"Avia Redding. She's living at the club. She was due back at Lokola, but her husband's ill at the clinic."

"And Dave has to nurse Mrs. Redding through her husband's illness. You'd have thought . . ."

Luke knew the rest of the sentence as if she had spoken it. "You'd have thought he'd have come to me first, if only from a sense of duty." He lengthened his pace so that she had to hurry a little.

"He's probably giving her a lift to a friend's house. I wouldn't mind betting that he'll be at the doctor's by the time we get there."

Luke would have lost his bet, but Tess had no

sooner brought him a drink to the porch than Dave did turn up, swinging back the gate and striding up the path with an arrogance that tugged at her nerves. With tensed sinews she bore his touch on her shoulder.

"Hello," she said, before he could speak. "Sweet of you to come as soon as you arrived."

Luke swallowed his brandy.

"Don't go, Luke," she said hastily. "I want a drink, too."

"Have it with Dave. I'll see you again before we go back. Good night, Tess."

When his footfalls had faded, Dave laid an arm across her shoulders. "Let's go inside."

In the lounge she drew away from him and shed her jacket. "Will you have whisky?"

"Later on. Don't you feel too good?"

"I feel fine." The emphasis was overdone.

He came to where she stood near the wine cabinet. "What are you worked up about? Haven't things been going right?"

"The doctor and his wife have been exceptionally kind, but I can't live with them any longer."

"I'm here till Monday. There's plenty of time to arrange something." His hand lifted as though to hold her wrist but she withdrew it swiftly. "I see. You'd rather not be touched," he remarked calmly. "I'll have that drink now, if you like."

She opened the cabinet and indicated where he would find bottle and glasses, crossed the room and sat down. He mixed his drink and tried it. Tess found her breath coming spasmodically; she wasn't ready for the tension of a scene with Dave. But there wouldn't be a scene. In her mind she could see him reasonably concluding that she'd had a rough time and was still on edge.

She watched him put down the glass and come round to rest upon the arm of another chair. He folded his arms and smiled at her.

"I believe it suits you better to wear your hair short like that. Reminds me of the first time I saw you."

"My face was different then," she said.

"Perhaps — rather more frank and clear. You never bothered to hide anything."

"I had nothing to hide."

"Is that meant as a kidney punch?" His tone remained even as he added: "I saw you out walking with Walt. I'd told him you weren't to go near town till tomorrow."

"Don't blame him. He had no option."

"I guessed that. You're a damned idiot."

"I know — and an inconvenient one." Her voice rose. "Dave, I must leave this district."

"I'm afraid you can't. I've given my word to Claud Kent to keep you either at Lokola or Fort Leppa. When this gun-running crowd are caught, you'll be called as a witness."

She paled. "But I don't have to stay all that while! A signed statement . . ."

"A statement under oath, remember. Would you sign yourself Teresa Paterson?" He paused, smiling slightly. "I thought not. The repercussions of a lightning decision such as the one I had to make on the night you arrived in Lokola can be hell, can't they? The simplest way out would be a quick trip to one of the ports down-river to persuade a missionary to marry us — but that would put you in a spot with Richard Barnwell."

"Fantastically funny," she said scathingly. "I think I've suffered enough at your hands."

His glance was mocking. "You didn't seem to object to them the other evening."

He was rewarded by a sweep of high colour which completely displaced her pallor.

"Only you would hurl a moment's weakness at me. Just then I'd have behaved the same with . . . Luke, or any other man." She leapt up and found him barring her way of escape. "Get out and leave me alone."

"Not yet, my sweet. And don't excite yourself, or I'll tell Greaves to order you back to bed." Thoughtfully, he went on: "I wonder if you and I will ever be able to talk together like two sensible human beings? Except for a brief interlude of madness we've spent most of the time we've been acquainted in baiting each other. You know why, don't you, Tess?"

Her chin came up. "Yes. We don't really like one another."

"You're wrong. From the beginning you challenged me. You were small and sweet, and tough and defiant — the queerest mixture I'd met in a girl. Your independence set my teeth on edge; your cheerful yielding up to your brothers of the money you earned maddened me."

She twisted and went over to a side table for cigarettes. "I thought you didn't care for exhumations."

"I don't. Since the Thursday night when Claud Kent handed over to me the green suit you'd been wearing and I knew you were in danger, I've admitted to myself that what we shared never died — it was buried alive."

He had casually followed her, taken the cigarette from her fingers and slipped it between his own lips. Without comment she selected another and struck a match. His cigarette jutted to the flame.

"Thank you, little one." Smoke spiralled from his sardonic mouth. "It must be nearly your bedtime, Teresa. Don't mind me. I'm waiting to have a word with Greaves. I'll be over tomorrow — probably after lunch. There's a meeting at head office in the morning."

"Bring Luke with you."

"Why? D'you feel more snug with him around? Walt has feelings, you know."

"Where I'm concerned they're nice ones — refreshingly so in this hothouse of the baser emotions. I'm not surprised that some of you go warped."

"Engaging child," he said. "Since we're being personal, you look like something from the native market in that dress. I'll try to get you a tailored one."

"Yes, do," she said coolly. "Ask Mrs. Redding to choose it. I'm sure she has perfect taste."

"That's an idea," he stated equably. "Good night."

CHAPTER SIX

THE north road from Fort Leppa ran straight across the burnt-up surface of Africa. At one of the villages they stopped to stretch their legs. Dave and Luke disinterestedly lounged in the shade of a rest-house while Tess roamed around.

As Tess came back to the rest-house Luke made room for her between himself and Dave on the wooden seat which flanked the back wall. There were only three walls: it reminded Tess of a primitive bus shelter.

"I wish we hadn't finished the drink," she said.

Dave regarded her with some displeasure. "You had it — a whole pint of lime water. If you weren't so restless you wouldn't be eternally thirsty."

Luke raised himself from the rickety bench. "I'll go and see if I can beg some sort of fruit. It'll help till we can buy a drink."

"Walt has tactfully left us alone," Dave murmured.

"Luke doesn't despair of keeping us out of the divorce court," she remarked.

Dave leant one arm along his crossed knee. "You'll have no bother in moving to the club tomorrow?"

"No. I don't possess much more than what I'm wearing."

"I'm hoping to put that right next week-end — you can't buy much here. I haven't seen you as often as I promised, but I've been busy . . . and that's not a cue for you to make a crack about Mrs. Redding."

"How's the sick husband?"

"Pretty bad. Avia is going with us to Lokola in the morning. She plans to empty the house and close it up."

"What will she do then?"

"If Redding gets well she'll take him home."

"But she's hoping he won't."

The corners of his mouth curled with distaste. "That's hardly the sort of comment I'd expect from you. Avia's having a tough time."

"I'm sorry." Her shoulders slumped. "When I came to Cape Ricos I almost prayed to hear that you were dead."

"I?" he said, startled.

She nodded moodily. "I thought death would take you right out of my life, and let me go wholeheartedly to Richard. I've never been . . . safe."

"Is that what you want?"

Her eyebrows lifted, a shade wearily. "Sometimes, though that wouldn't be a bit important if I were happy. How did I manage to make such a muddle of my life?"

"Men," he said laconically. "There's something in

you that makes you tackle them two or three at a time. I hope Richard is jealous and possessive. That's the only way he'll keep you."

"I'm not going to marry Richard."

"No?" There was no astonishment in the query. "Well, maybe he's better off that way."

"I suppose you wouldn't take me with you tomorrow?" she asked.

"You suppose right."

"You said the danger is over."

"So it is. The gun-running has been stopped and the police have arrested two Portuguese who were selling the stuff to native chiefs."

"What about that man?"

"You won't be called as a witness against him, after all. It seems to be a clear-cut case. He'll probably be fined heavily for certain contraventions of the law and kicked out of the country."

"Rather a tame ending to so much excitement." She bent to pick up a twig and trace lines with it on the floor. "I didn't think you'd let him get away with trying to poison me."

"I didn't," he said casually. "I shot him in the hip."

The twig dropped. For a long moment Tess was still, gazing close at the pattern she had drawn. Her heart seemed to be hammering into her thigh and her throat at the same time. She straightened up.

"When?"

"The day after I found you in the forest. I hadn't dared to use natives in the search for you in case the alarm should be given—in which event you'd doubtless have come to a hasty and violent end. But once you were virtually under lock and key I turned some boys loose. We found the remains of the shack, and cars tracks led along a concealed path. Then we came across the car itself; it was smothered by vines and branches, which I noticed had been literally torn from the earth and the trees only a short while before. It was easy to follow him a mile or two into the undergrowth, and when I did come up with him, crouching among ferns, I let him have it."

She made a small sound of sick distress. "He was like a trapped animal. Need you have done it?"

"I'm afraid so, Teresa. I felt decidedly better afterwards."

"I'm glad you didn't kill him. I'm sure he was fundamentally decent." She pressed a clammy hand over her eyes. "Why didn't you tell me before?"

"We've hardly been alone since I arrived last Thursday. Besides, I knew you'd be disgusted—your whole sense of values is cockeyed."

After a minute she got up and went to the opening of the rest-house. About a hundred yards away, in the shade of a bokungu tree, Luke sat surrounded by coconuts. He was piercing holes and emptying the milk into the metal cap from the thermos flask.

"It seems that I'm free to leave West Africa," she said thinly.

Dave shifted. "If you care to wait a month we can all leave in style."

She turned and regarded him queerly. "Is this another joke?"

"Not at all. At the company meeting on Friday morning I resigned—gave a month's notice. The usual notice is three months, but I slipped into the job without a contract. Brig can do what he likes with my share of the tin mine. When Walt hears that I'm finishing here he'll wind up, too."

She held on to an ant-ridden post. "Where are you going?"

"As far as I can get from tin miners and alluvial deposits."

"And citrus farms?"

He stood up and dug his hands into his pockets. "Last time I left Lokola my ideas were beautifully definite — to kick around the world for a year and settle on a farm in a good climate for the rest of my life. They fell in like a rotten roof. This time I'm making no plans, but I shan't come back."

"Why did you ask me to hang on till you leave — for the look of the thing?"

"No, Teresa," he said mockingly. "Seeing that we're considered to be related, it would cause no comment if you decided to come along with us."

Tess had to take her time about answering that. But finally she said, "You forgot to give me a jade and diamond ring first, Dave," and walked out to join Luke.

To please him she swallowed some of the tepid liquid he offered her. She was recalling the first talk she had had with Luke, his offhand statement that Dave would never forgive her for letting him go. At the time she had believed she understood what he had in mind, but now she was less sure.

She would get nowhere by fighting with Dave; he had her beaten every time. Even when she ran away he had been forced to come after her and drag her out of a mess. The rare tenderness which had surprised her at Zinto and drawn out all her own yielding sweetness might never have existed. He could still be gentle, but only from pity. Viciousness cloaked in mockery composed his general mood. For Tess it did have the pride-saving effect of keeping emotionalism at bay. There would be no more lapses.

Upon his suggestion of five minutes ago she dared not ponder just yet. She did not doubt that beneath the sarcasm lay a serious invitation, but a stuffy, glaring village with a background of native chatter and chanting was scarcely the best place in which to debate it.

On the return journey Tess sat in the back of the car; it happened as naturally as if it had been agreed to.

The car dipped alongside a wide rift, product of soil erosion yet prodigally green; wound up a hill, and from its summit they saw Fort Leppa, arching spears of palms above walls and cupolas—a picture postcard painting in the smouldering glow of sunset.

Dave drove round to the back of the club.

"Coming in, Tess?" Luke asked.

"It'll be noisy at the bar," Dave said. "I'll bring a drink out here."

Luke smiled at her from the footpath. "So long. I shan't be down next week-end, but perhaps Dave will bring you back with him."

She returned some banality, and her eyes followed the two figures till they disappeared; or rather they followed the tall, broad-shouldered figure while her lips smiled wryly, without humour.

Dave brought her a long drink which sparkled amber. It prickled in her nostrils and created a warmth in her chest. He had edged into the driver's seat but was half-facing her, as though interestedly awaiting developments.

"Is it good?"

"Mmm. What is it?"

"A panacea for misery, but unfortunately not a cure. Don't take to drinking that while you're alone at the club. And one other thing." He smiled slightly but spoke with a deliberation which was intended to impress. "There are very few women here—not more than fifteen in the whole town, and most of them live in the residential quarter. Your bedroom is on a private corridor, and I've made sure that the bells are in order, but you must take the precaution of locking your door every night."

"Spoken like an affectionate husband," she said flippantly. "Don't worry. No one will ever seduce me against my will."

"Don't be so clever. You pleaded to be allowed to leave the doctor's house for something more lively, and I agreed on condition that you're careful." He took her glass and placed it on the floor of the car. "How are you off for ready cash?"

"I'll manage."

"You can buy anything you like at the store and charge it to my account."

"I suspect your generosity, Dave."

"You would," he said, in cold clipped accents, "but your suspicions have even less basis than they had before."

He twisted back and started the car. It swerved out and climbed one of the steep avenues. At the Greaves' house he got out to give her a hand.

"I won't come in," he said. "Sure you've got all you need?"

"Quite. Thanks for the afternoon out. You certainly provided a couple of highlights."

The warning sparks were visible in his grey eyes, but he spoke without heat. "Think it over, Teresa. I can put you on a plane to the Cape, where you'll be lonely and more restless than ever, or we needn't part yet. If you decide to throw in with Walt and me, there'll be no strings, except of your own making. Have your answer ready by next Saturday. I'll say goodbye now."

She stood motionless, incapable of a spontaneous smile, as the car purred away. The house, when she entered, was quiet, except for the muted movements of the kitchen boy. She went into her bedroom, adjusted the mosquito screen over the window, drew the curtains against the fast-encroaching dusk, and snapped on a light.

Her reflection stared from the mirror, thin and shadowed, her eyes uncommonly large and dark. Like a machine, her mind revolved its problem. Dave was leaving the tropics, and she believed him when he stated that this time there would be no turning back. Dare she hope that good would come of accepting his invitation? Didn't the fact that he had asked her prove, in itself, that whatever power she had wielded over him had by now been thoroughly sapped? Otherwise he couldn't have tolerated her proximity.

She experienced a sudden, horrified palpitation of the heart. Dave wasn't acting. He really did feel that way— cold and embittered. No woman would ever rouse him again as she had at Zinto. That was why he could contemplate several weeks in her company with equanimity. It also explained his chilly reaction when, in fright and weakness, she had begged the solace of his arms.

What had she done to him?

Tess was trembling with an agonizing sensation. She had been striving to reach something in him which she herself had destroyed. Surely there was some way of atoning.

At the moment, in her new awareness, Tess could not sort it out. She only knew she was bound to go wherever he went so long as he would suffer her nearness.

CHAPTER SEVEN

CAPE RICOS was a small, ramshackle port. The waterfront was a straggle of cement and wooden structures, all in need of repair, and except for a scraggy palm here and there the couple of streets of houses were hardly more prepossessing.

There were few boats at the quay just now. A couple of cargo boats, an oil carrier and a nicely rigged ketch which belonged to a rubber-estate owner from Loanda. From where Dave had camped they could look down over thorn and berry trees to the hot grey Atlantic. The tent had been erected in the shade of some tamarind trees which Dave said had originally been brought from India for their medicinal properties by Portuguese monks. From the sea came a ceaseless wind which lost its heat soon after sunset and made a blanket necessary overnight. Sleeping in the tent was the only part of this camping venture which Tess disliked. She would far rather have lain outdoors in a sleeping-bag near Dave and Luke, and watched the stars till she could stay awake no longer. But Dave wouldn't hear of it.

"You'll crawl under canvas each night at ten and stay there till dawn," he'd stated flatly. "I don't care if you do wear pants and short hair—you're still a woman . . . very much so."

"I can't sleep properly shut in like that," she had protested.

To which he had replied: "Walt and I wouldn't sleep properly outside if you were there, so it's two against one. You must make up your mind to get used to it."

She had given in. During the last six weeks, since Dave had put the proposition in the ant-infested rest-house, giving in had developed into a habit with Tess.

They had left Fort Leppa a week ago. Apart from the time it took to acquire the necessary equipment there had been the matter of Francis Redding's death. Upon Dave's advice, Avia had gone to friends of hers somewhere along the coast, and he and Luke had cleared up Redding's accounts.

On their arrival at Cape Ricos she had had some luck. Her trunk, which she had presumed lost in the coastal vessel that had brought her here, had been unloaded, and left in the customs shed. Damp had got into her clothes, and the odour of it seemed ineradicable, but there they were, the gay beach frocks and slacks from Lourenço Marques, the tailored linens from England and a cosmopolitan array of footwear.

Luke was less put out by the feminine clutter than he had anticipated. Indeed, he missed it when it was all packed away again and his own and Dave's under-clothes hung on the line each day. There were seldom any of Tess's, so he took it that she hardly ever wore any.

Luke would have liked things to come right for Tess—she was so game, so completely unaffected—but he was glad she had the tent to herself; it would have un-settled him had Dave shared it with her. As it was, they managed admirably.

During the day the men fished and read. When the weather cooled they would all three go down by the footpath into the town and perhaps play tennis or squash. Invariably they were invited to one of the houses for a meal, and when they trudged back in the darkness, Tess would take an arm of each and breathe fast as she kept up with their long strides.

They would sit up for an hour, watching the spitting fire and discussing the sort of subject that goes with darkness and comradeship.

About noon each day the men brought the fish to the camp and Tess, who spent the mornings lazily, would become energetic and housewifely.

One morning it rained; nothing violent, but it was depressing to have to sit in the tent or in a car while the men went fishing. The warm, slate-colored drizzle shrouded everything; from the car she could not see the tent, a dozen yards away. The fireplace was a sod-den mass of grey ash. Egrets and gulls were grounded, and the usual roar of the waves had become reduced to a sibilant whisper.

Towards lunch-time it cleared and the world began to steam. Tess had got into a swim-suit and was pulling on sandals when the men arrived.

"Coming?" she asked, not very cordially. They never invited her to go fishing.

Luke said a brief, "No, thanks," and lowered to his haunches to clear out the fireplace.

Dave said: "We've been in, but I'll walk down with you. The mist is bad below, and the path is tricky."

She draped a bath towel across her shoulders and started off ahead of him. He caught her up and grasped her elbow, and they carried on together down the path. At the overhang the track narrowed, and his shoulder slid naturally behind hers while his hand moved to her waist.

Prompted by the firmness of his touch and his air of impregnability, she said with a slightly vicious emphasis, "Remember when we used to bathe in your pool at Zinto?"

"I do," he admitted evenly. "You're the only woman I've ever kissed under water."

"I must enter that in my diary alongside the sock on the jaw." She paused. "I still don't see why you had to abandon the farm so abruptly. You didn't intend to when you left. Your only aim was to drive me off the property, and that happened within a week or so of your departure."

"Zinto was Paterson's Folly."

"Was it, though?" She slanted him a glance. "Tess Bentley, too?"

"Yes—but I was coming back to you."

She stopped dead, her face lifted and drained of blood. "You . . . were?"

"Don't get emotional. It's over now."

Her fingers curled tight over his sleeve. "But, Dave . . . why didn't you?"

"Arnold wrote that you'd left the district and were going to England. It seemed that you weren't even going to hang on to see if I did turn up." He shrugged. "We were finished, so I got dug back into Lokola."

"Oh." It was a sound of resignation and pain. She turned slowly and walked on. "As you say, it's over now."

"We're two changed people," he added.

Tess made no answer. Her nerves were suddenly raw and smarting, and all she desired was to be away from him for a while.

"I'll go on alone, Dave. Don't wait for me."

She broke into a run, which finished at the low sand-dunes at the back of the beach, left towel and sandals in a heap and dived straight into a wave. The midday heat of the sun was increasing the mist. She surfaced in a white vapour and swam about, fiercely aware of the cool sting of the water and the sense of being withdrawn from the aches and stabs of life.

Yet it was not long before the bitterness and irony

ran together in her veins like a toxin. Some things are impossible to bear. Had he spoken gently, or even less dispassionately, the shock of grief might have been somewhat tempered. He had actually intended coming back to her . . .

"Tess!"

He must have followed. Why shouldn't he let her lose herself in the mist? No one would care. Lethargically, she swam in, stood up on the beach and pressed her hair away from her forehead. He materialized at her side.

"I was afraid you'd go the wrong way and get bogged in the silt."

"I'd have stayed there till the sun came out," she told him ungraciously. "It's a hell of a job for a strong swimmer to drown."

He flung the towel round her and bent to push on her sandals. "Let's hope Walt's got the fire going. This damp is no good to anyone. Another day like this and we'll have to break camp and move on."

Tess did not enquire where to. She stood on a rock, kicked her feet free of sand and began a quick return up the path. Her heart pounded and her mouth was stiff; she wasn't sure what she would do if Dave touched her again.

Luke had not only started a fire, but fillets of fish were cooking in a pan of palm-oil, and he was setting the table for three. Up here the moisture had evaporated and a clean sun burned directly overhead. Through the tamarinds it shed a python-skin pattern of black and gold. By the time Tess had rubbed down and dressed, the fish and a pot of coffee were ready.

Mid-afternoon, the sea came right out of the mist, calm as polished pewter under the steel-blue sky. A cargo vessel went out under steam, leaving a dark, white-fringed wedge in its wake, and shortly afterwards a liner crossed the mouth of the bay.

"She's not stopping," Luke said, in the odd expressionless voice he had acquired since yesterday.

"Bound for Kanos," Dave commented. "That's what you can do with, Walt—a spell in Kanos."

"Why don't we buy a boat and go?"

Desultorily, the men discussed all the gear necessary

for a cruise down the coast. They talked about the design of the ketch *Bondoa,* her masts and sails, the ballasting and food storage capacity. Tess listened, knowing that Dave was merely talking to pass the time. His manner was conversational and without purpose.

No rain came next day, but a film hung over the sea and the outriggers stayed close to the shore. The camp had too strong an atmosphere of hangover, so when Dave and Luke had set out with their tackle, Tess made her way down to the waterfront and spent a couple of hours in the shade of a tree, reading. She got back in time to mix a batter and open a tin of luncheon beef. When the men strolled up she was ready to serve the slices of meat fried in batter, and hot beans.

Luke, as he doused his face at the bucket, was actually smiling. He came to the table wiping his hands.

"Hope you're going to be a good sailor, Tess."

She hesitated, dish in hand, became aware of Dave at her back, and went on loading the plates.

"Are you telling me that you've bought the *Bondoa?*"

"Dave has. We're taking over at once and can sail as soon as the papers are in order."

She ladled beans for Luke and placed the dish near Dave. "Have you ever sailed in a ketch, Luke?"

"I was a member of the yacht club at Massa, but there we floated round a lagoon. Dave did some cruising in a yawl when he went wandering a year or two back, and we've taken on the present crew of three Portuguese. One of them is a first-class navigator, and one can cook, so we'll get through all right."

Tess wasn't so sure. Once on the high seas in the seventy foot *Bondoa* there would be no way of escape. And anyway, Dave might feel the same distaste for her as she felt for him. She ate a little, but remained outside the conversation about the purchase.

When lunch was cleared and Luke had disappeared to change his shirt, Dave looked up from a sheaf of forms he had spread over the table.

"You'd better come down this afternoon and choose your cabin. The small one is more private — the other one has to be used as lounge and dining-room too."

"You're sure you want me on the boat?"

"Of course we're taking you with us."

55   161

"Very well. My only stipulation," she said, avoiding his eyes, "is a cabin with a door that locks."

His mouth set. "You shall have it. And you'll need some kind of wardrobe rigged up."

"Don't bother—yet. If I don't take to sailing I'll be leaving you at Kanos. How soon can we start sleeping on the boat?"

"We'll break camp tomorrow. We're selling both cars."

Luke ranged over, his eyes crinkled with pleasure. "I'll feel bad saying goodbye to my bus, but these fellows in Cape Ricos can't get 'em. And it'll be great to have a new one some time."

Two or three days ago Tess would have become saddened at the drawing of tent-pegs, the stacking away of chairs and china and pots. But her only sensation the following afternoon was one of relief. She got into Dave's car, and when they jolted up round the hill and down to the earth road on the other side she had no urge to look back.

For three days the Portuguese seamen worked on freshening the ship. They cleaned and varnished the booms and masts, gave the outside a coat of white paint down to the gunmetal grey waterline, repaired the sails and oiled the deck. The cabins were white-enamelled with a stained teak trim, and the engine-room and galley were finished in grey. The *Bondoa* was roomy and well-built; there was even deck space for cargo had they cared to turn traders.

As Tess grew accustomed to the feel of the deck beneath her flat, rubber-soled sandals and came to know one Portuguese from another, her heart lightened. There was an infectious excitement about sailing in a ship like the *Bondoa*. Luke and Dave were busy cleaning the engine and fitting a renovated exhaust, checking the ballast and acquiring gear and extra tools in the most unexpected places.

The fourth day a hundred and fifty gallons of water and food stores for a fortnight came aboard. The cold-storage plant was filled out with vegetables, fruit and dressed chickens. Then the gear was stowed and the seamen slung their hammocks aft. At about five the dinghy was hoisted and the lines cast loose. A collection of natives on the quay set up a racket, dancing so near the edge that a couple fell into the water.

Under power the *Bondoa* backed. The sails filled in the westerly breeze, white canvas touched with the ochre of a dying, brazen sun. Tess stood with her feet wide to watch the receding land. A miraculous coolness encompassed her, fresh salt air which reached and cleansed the sore places of her mind.

At her side Dave remarked laconically: "There goes Cape Ricos. Never no more!"

"The air's a tonic," she said.

"We can do with it. Go and put on a sweater."

By dusk they were well out and moving down the thick green coast of Africa, which was vanishing under a purple pall from the east. The sky was clear and packed with birds which were homing to the rocks. A consistent wind persuaded Dave to cut out the engine, and quietly the *Bondoa* rode the billowing waters.

Shortly after dawn on their third morning out, Tess took her sea-water bath and came on deck. The *Bondoa* was anchored close inshore, and she could see an iron building and the tops of native huts among the dozens of coconut palms. Past the settlement mangroves clawed into the mouth of a black, tunnelled river.

She glanced along the deck to where Dave stood shaving at an unsteady mirror.

"Badoun," he called in explanation. "Copra and palm-oil station."

"Are you going ashore?"

"D'you want to?"

"I shan't come this way again."

He towelled his jaws and walked down to where she was standing. "I'll take you over after breakfast. The village isn't much, but there are some rare trees." He pointed. "See those orchids in the treetops?"

"I can't see anything for palms."

"Just above those low ones."

She shook her head, and he bent to bring his eyes level with hers.

"No, you're not tall enough." He moved his face against her hair and sniffed. "You smell nice, Teresa."

"Thank you."

"If you'd turn your lips a little I could kiss you."

163

"You're in a generous mood this morning."

"The sea makes a man doubly conscious of women—didn't you know that?"

"Did you know it—before we came?"

He laughed. "I took a chance. After all, you're the only woman around and I've had to be conscious of you for some weeks now, so the risk wasn't enormous." A pause. "No kiss?"

"Not just now."

"We'll have to get by on coffee, then. Come and have it with Walt."

When the dinghy was lowered, Luke elected to remain aboard. He'd seen enough bug-holes like Badoun, and the reek of palm-oil was quite penetrating enough from the boat. So Dave and Tess went alone, and tied up the dinghy among the mangrove roots. The scene was one which Tess had always expected to encounter in this part of Africa. Flowers were pasted all over the place on the dark foliage which rioted between the trees. The river cascaded over boulders and pushed streams of white froth under the arched roots of kapok and mahogany, and from every crevice in every tree-trunk issued a network of ferns and mosses, vines and creepers. The whole place dripped, beating on the broad leaves of the lower vegetation in a continuous rain.

Dave went to the water's edge and peered upwards. "You get a good view of those orchids from here."

She joined him. "I wonder how they take root, among leaves? Uncanny and beautiful, isn't it?" She shivered. "This place reminds me of the house among the trees, except that there it was terribly dark . . . and hopeless."

"Don't dwell on it. Any place is hopeless when you're alone and unhappy."

She let a few seconds elapse. "That sounds rather a drastic confession, from you."

"It's true of most people. The being alone is the worst. When two people are unhappy together there's an element of hope which blunts the edge of the bitterness."

"Is this an abstract discussion?"

"Not entirely."

She turned from him slightly and pulled at a long, sawtoothed leaf. "You're not unhappy, Dave. Perhaps you were when you left Zinto but you're not now. You haven't that much feeling."

"If it's gone," he said curtly, "you killed it."

"It succumbed without a struggle, through a jealousy which you knew to be groundless."

"Jealousy had nothing to do with it! You didn't understand me—you don't yet."

Piccanins were swarming over the dinghy. Dave scattered them with a spate of profanity and a few coins. His smile, as he rowed to the *Bondoa,* had an irritating twist of cynicism, and Tess knew again the unbearable ache of defeat.

An hour later, with a steady breeze raising ripples on the waves, the *Bondoa* got under way. Badoun melted back into the rich coastline.

That evening Tess asked:

"How soon do we arrive at Kanos?"

"Tomorrow afternoon, if we keep up this speed."

"Are we staying there several days?"

"It's a city of women and wine, Teresa—more wine than women. Walt will have to decide how long we stay."

Luke said: "That's laying it on a bit thick. I could get tight aboard if I hankered to."

Dave grinned, but made no further comment.

Kanos was a city of intense heat and gaiety. The club, the most palatial along the coast, sustained a fairly high pitch of excitement by frequent gala dinners and celebrations, and the Polo Club ran two first-class teams. Then there were the races and the river, and a vast amount of social life surrounding the Governor's residence.

Tess liked the sparkling town and most of the people she encountered. She was amazed by their hospitality, and it was pleasant, too, to be admired and pursued for dances. She became acquainted with a few wives and found them a little less licentious than she had anticipated. One or two were blatant in their infidelity, but the rest, though of one voice in their detestation of the tropics, were normal in most respects. Apparently the weary ones were too exhausted to come out in search of distraction. Tess heard about them, but did not meet them.

Those days in Kanos provided the diversion which Tess needed. She returned to the *Bondoa* in the early hours of each morning almost too tired to undress and tumble into her bunk and she slept so late that when she sauntered out into the sunshine breakfast was over and the men had gone off to town or boarded a cargo vessel for a yarn with the skipper.

The mornings were long and restful. Lying under the awning on deck she could watch the Negro dock labourers or the busy plying of a launch. Invariably she got so drugged with heat that she dozed till the men leapt on deck, and Dave stirred her with his toe and called her a slacker.

Tess had decided that while so much was available to occupy her thoughts, she would exclude Dave from them as far as possible. That was why she so eagerly accepted invitations which did not include him. Yet always, at the back of her mind, lay the conviction that they were nearing the end.

At Fort Leppa, while awaiting his intimation that he and Luke were at last unfettered and ready to travel, she had imagined that to be permitted to live near him and bear his masculine moods was the ultimate of her desires. Dave himself, with masculine brutality, had shattered that particular illusion; but it would be time enough to lay herself bare when be began to talk of leaving Kanos.

When she came on deck the fifth morning, Luke was caulking a seam near the companionway.

"Hello," she said, dropping down to sit on her heels. "Let me do some of that."

"Go and get your breakfast."

"I had all I want in the cabin. Club dinners last me nearly all day. Can I dip out the tar?"

"No." He poked a black mass into a few inches of the crevice with a kitchen knife. "Those johnnies you dance with ought to see you now."

"What a wonderful idea! Why don't we give a deck party?"

"Dave wouldn't hear of it. At least, I hope he wouldn't."

"Is he in the cabin?"

"No. He's gone to bail out Gomes—he was in a fight last night."

Idly she stirred the inch or so of tar in the bottom of the can. "I'm going to ask Dave about giving a party— one of those bohemian things when you sit around on deck and eat mounds of savouries. We could get the seamen to play and sing."

"He won't have it. He couldn't stand the thought of a lot of careless beggars treading out cigarettes all over the planks and poking their noses into the cabins."

"It's no worse than entertaining a gang of people in one's house."

"A boat is more of a novelty to strangers than a house." Luke was carefully smoothing off the job and scraping up the surplus smears of tar. "I'd forget it if I were you."

"We've accepted so many invitations."

"You can give a dinner at the club. Dave would prefer that."

She pressed several thumb-prints along the repaired seam. "I suppose you're right. You know him awfully well, don't you, Luke?"

He shrugged. "I know that he has a fanatical pride in his own possessions, that he can't tolerate sharing anything. He's always been that way. He wouldn't even let me go halves with the boat."

She sat back with her legs crossed under her, rested an elbow on her knee and her chin in her hand. Her tones were oddly flat. "He owned half the mine with Brigham."

"He hadn't any affection for the mine or for Brigham —never did have. It was just a bond with Lokola." Luke became absorbed in the unnecessary task of straightening the edges of a seam adjacent to the one he had caulked. "Remember our first conversation — when I said he'd never forgive you for letting him go?"

She nodded. "I've often tried to get at what you meant. He . . . we did love each other, Luke. I misunderstood his motives about something rather vital and he retaliated by demanding what seemed an impossibility. I was terribly unwise, and he was intolerant."

"So you quarrelled good and hot and that was that. Yet I'll wager that at the time you could have got anything out of Dave by giving in. He's a tougher proposition now."

She breathed a dispirited sigh, and stared silently at the emerald islands off the coast.

"You see," said Luke reasonably, "you didn't only twist his heart. The way he saw it you also wrecked his life's ambition. For either, Dave would flail himself like hell so long as you got your share of chastisement, too. Something will snap in him one day—you'll just have to wait for it."

There were a few things about Dave that even Luke hadn't guessed at, thought Teresa broodingly. He moved on with his tin of tar, and she got up and wandered along to the main cabin in search of reading-matter. Sitting at the long table against the wall, she leafed through a pile of periodicals. But she had never had the faculty for concentrating on magazine stories, even tough ones like these. An article on African timbers reminded her, by some swift and roundabout train of thought, of Martin Cramer, and she wondered if there were anyone else who ever spared a memory for the tragic young man. She saw that his early end had been as inevitable as the stars. There is no niche anywhere for the spiritually frightened people of this world.

At a sound behind her she turned, and shifted up to sit on the table with a foot on a chair.

"The skipper himself," she said. "Did you hook Gomes out of jail?"

"I did." Dave sloughed his jacket and slipped undone another button of his shirt. "Isn't he back?"

"Maybe. I've been reading." Sensing an unmistakable change in him, Tess became uneasy. "Is it very hot in town this morning?"

"Like a blast furnace."

He lit a cigarette and stood gazing through the porthole at the blue and white combers rolling towards the sand bar.

"D'you want me to go?" she asked.

"No, I've something to tell you." He looked at her, his grey eyes keen yet so dark as to cause her a qualm of foreboding. "We're taking on another passenger."

"Are we? What kind?"

"It's Avia Redding."

Slowly Tess reached her feet to the floor. "How nice," she said. "In which case you'll still be three."

"I guessed you'd say that, but you're not running out, Tess. I met Avia this morning. She was having coffee at the club; it's the first time she's walked since landing in Kanos over a week ago. She's a sick woman."

"Kanos has a nursing-home."

"Not for her kind of sickness. You've never even met Avia. Why do you dislike her so much?"

Tess answered abruptly, "Perhaps because she's in love with you."

"She isn't, but if she were it wouldn't make any difference. I'm so placed that I'm bound to help her."

"Go ahead then, but don't expect me to make friends with your ex-mistress."

He drew a thick breath. "You're about as sweet to handle as a swordfish. Avia is Redding's widow, and I was Redding's friend for a number of years."

"So was Luke, but I'll bet he's not nearly so anxious to have her aboard as you are. It's all right, Dave," with a mock-jaunty shrug she dipped her hands into the pockets of her shorts and took a step nearer the door, "bring the woman here, by all means. I'll take care to leave the cabin neat and tidy."

In a couple of strides he had closed the door and was standing with his back to it. "I'm not fighting with you, Tess. For once in my life I'm appealing to you. I'm asking you to do something for me."

His strange tautness, the unfamiliar angle of his chiselled mouth, set a pain working about her heart

"What is it?" she said. "To share the cabin with Mrs Redding, to help her back to the woman she was when you drove her around Fort Leppa?" She paused and went on shakily. "If you cared for me as you did at Zinto, I might point a parallel. Martin was sick, too . . ."

"There's no comparison. You were under no obligation to help Cramer—the reverse, in fact." He came over, hand outstretched to grip her elbow. "You're making this much too important, but I knew you would, though for the life of me I couldn't see how else to act.

169

Avia can sleep in here and Walt and I will make do with hammocks on deck. We'll cruise up to Madeira—take our time about it so that she gets fit—and put her on a boat for England. There's nothing more to it, Tess."

Her head was bent away from him. "Don't pretend that she means so little to you. Just meeting her this morning has altered you. I'm sorry, Dave. If she comes aboard the *Bondoa* I shall have to go."

He compelled her into his arms, not fiercely but with half-angry force. He raised her chin, and held back his head.

"Regard it this way," he said. "Avia is a burden we both have to bear for a while. I'm bringing her here this evening but we shan't sail till Friday. Promise you'll give it a trial."

In the circle of Dave's arms, with his breath warm and smoky across her cheek and the muscles of his shoulders hard beneath her hands, Tess would have agreed to anything.

A knock came at the door and he let her go. Luke hesitated on the threshold and walked in.

"Came for my pipe," he said.

"You may as well stay to hear the news," Dave replied evenly. "Mrs. Redding is joining us this evening for a week or two."

Luke assumed a blank mask. "That'll be grand. I think I'll stroll up to the Boulevard for some tobacco."

"Take Tess with you. She needs some exercise before lunch."

That afternoon, in her cabin, Tess made valiant attemps to straighten her thoughts. From whatever angle she contemplated them, the days ahead prickled with danger. She had heard enough about Avia Redding to be in no doubt as to that woman's emotions towards her late husband. Unwittingly, Luke had let fall some time ago that Avia had been attracted to Dave, and Tess, being a woman in love, had tormentingly stored that information and occasionally reviewed it.

She believed that Dave and Avia had never been lovers, but there was nothing to prove that they hadn't wanted to be. And what about the stressed "obligation" towards her? Wasn't it possible that he had made promises and had to retract them when his "wife" inconveniently turned up? The very suggestion was insupportable.

The sun went down and Kanos sprang alive, its lights hung out in uneven tiers along the waterfront and the avenues above. Mingling with the smells of cordage and spice came the faint aroma of *frangipani*. The breeze must be blowing off the land.

Luke appeared and made fast the short gangway up to the quay. The use of this was something new. When Tess went ashore she stood on the side of the boat, grabbed someone's hand and leapt up to the jetty; she could slither down to the deck unaided.

"Now we look like a real ship," she said aloud.

"If we'd taken the trouble to put it there for you, you wouldn't have used it," he countered dourly. "Trouble with you is you take everything as a challenge."

"One has to, in a hostile world." She smiled without much humour. "You needn't be afraid that I'll challenge Mrs. Redding."

His glance was suspicious. His mouth began to open, but apparently he decided on discretion and closed it again. On tiptoes, he peered over the edge of the quay.

"Here comes a taxi. It'll be Dave."

Tess pushed back her chair. Annoyed to find her knees uncertain, she took a fresh hold of herself and backed slightly in order to watch the arrival. Dave got out of the taxi, paid off, and then helped Avia from the back seat.

Tess hadn't formed any picture of the woman; she had merely recalled the regular ivory features turned upon Dave in an intimate and knowledgeable smile. Vaguely she had thought Mrs. Redding would be sheathed in black with a touch of white at the neck, that she would smile sadly and lean upon Dave. Certainly she was unprepared for the thin creature in scarlet with garish circles of rouge on the prominent white cheek-bones, and dark eyes restless and fever-bright.

Involuntary, she stepped forward to lend a hand as the woman reached the foot of the gangway. Dave was smiling politely—just as if, fumed Tess to herself, he were not almost carrying Avia Redding. On the deck

Avia paused, ignoring Luke. Her interest centred upon the head of pale curls and the honey-tan face. She spoke in a small, dead voice.

"So you're Dave's wife. You're the reason I'm ill and unwanted . . ."

Smoothly, Dave interrupted. "You're not unwanted, Avia, and Tess has nothing to do with your being ill."

"She has everything to do with it . . . everything."

"Come and lie down," he said, "and the cook will fix you a meal."

Tess was trembling. She sought behind her, found a boom for support and let it have her weight.

Luke muttered: "She's just sick, Tess. Take no notice. Dave will be back soon and we three will eat together on deck."

"How dare he bring her here," she breathed. "How dare he!"

"You don't understand."

But Tess had twisted suddenly, almost frenziedly, at the sound of a klaxon.

"Hey there, Tess!" a man called. "Have you forgotten our party? Where's Dave?"

"He's busy," she panted. "But I'll come."

Luke snatched at her wrist. "You can't, Tess."

"Can't I?" Like a vixen she wrenched free. "If Dave wants me back he'd better come for me at midnight." And she was up the gangway and flying towards the car.

But as the anchor light of the *Bondoa* dimmed out, her whole being crumpled. That frightful woman . . . and her ghostly voice! Most of all her voice.

CHAPTER EIGHT

THAT night Tess occupied the spare bedroom in the house of a young married government inspector. The suggestion was Dave's. He had arrived at the party in the club just before eleven, and within five minutes had become convinced that Tess was too strung up to face the night on the boat. For one thing she could scarcely bear to look at him, and she shivered and turned away when he asked her to dance.

So at midnight she found herself in the back of a saloon car, with Dave saying good night to her at the window. Several drinks had dulled the shock but made her sleepy and wretched.

In her room on the Boulevard she slept heavily, and it was with a sense of loss and fear that she awakened late in strange surroundings. Her head ached and her mouth had the raw flavour of stale smoke. A houseboy brought tea and a parcel which contained her pink linen frock. Dave had sent it down, with a note pinned under the lapel.

Walt will pick you up at twelve and take you to lunch and polo. Stick with him, there's a good girl, and try not to hate me too much.

She reeled from bedroom to bathroom and back again, put on the frock and brushed her hair. It was already ten o'clock, but her hostess still lay sleeping. In search of fresh air she went out to the verandah, but apparently the light wind still blew off the land. It smelled sickly and damp. She sat down and her head throbbed into the cushion against which it rested. It was a headache such as she had never before experienced, a blinding, dizzying illness of the brain.

Her hostess had just trailed out in a dressing-gown and said good morning when an impeccably attired Luke drove up in a taxi. Good morning merged into goodbye and thanks, and Tess got into the ancient vehicle and closed her eyes against the bumps as it rolled down towards the club.

"Rocky?" queried Luke. "Is it a hangover?"

"And how," she said faintly.

"Taken anything?"

"Not even an aspirin. There was no one about and I had no money."

"Filthy luck. We'll put you right at the club."

He seated her in the thick shade of the club terrace and brought her two tablets and a bromo-seltzer. In a little while her keel evened, but she remained pale and listless. At one o'clock Luke insisted that they go for lunch.

While they were eating, he said: "Dave and I didn't

173

sleep on the boat last night. He said I was to be sure and tell you that."

"What difference would it have made if you had?"

"Not much, but you might have wondered. We spent most of the night playing cards on the *Mercury*. Dave said—"

"I'd rather not hear it, Luke."

"You've got to confront the facts some time."

"But I have to assimilate a few others first. I'm afraid they're too horrible to take at one gulp."

"That's foolish, and very unjust."

"I can't help it. At the moment I feel that I never want to see Dave or the *Bondoa* again."

"Hell! Whatever he's done he did for you." In his exasperation Luke shoved away his half-finished pudding. "I made myself believe hard things about him, too, but you've got to hand it to him when he's in a spot. You don't suppose it feels good to have Mrs. Redding slung about his neck, do you?"

Tess raised an unsteady hand to her forehead. "Please let's leave it, Luke. I need some coffee."

During the afternoon Luke did his utmost to be normal and companionable. He drove her out to the river mouth where they could watch natives hollowing canoes from mahogany logs and the women washing *cassava* roots. They came back to a Hausa store and he made her select for him a couple of ties.

"I may use a tie more often when we're settled," he told her. "I'm not going to be one of your shirt-and-trousers store owners. It's time I started living."

"Is seafaring already getting you down?"

"No, but I'll be glad to have a place of my own."

"Aren't you ever going to marry?"

"Ever's a long time, but the more I put it off the more remote the chance. The tropics have spoiled me for the domestic life. Apart from trying to make a man over and filling his rooms with junk, a woman can be the devil of a nuisance."

"You don't have to choose the managing kind."

"The gentle ones go in for big families, and that wouldn't suit me, either. I'd be content to watch Dave's kids grow up."

Tess contrived a distorted smile and came out of the shop ahead of him.

"Now we'll go straight to the boat," he said.

She shook her head. "No, Luke."

"You're not still scared?"

"I'm just not up to it."

"Up to what? You simply go to your cabin and get some rest. I promised Dave I'd bring you back."

"That woman will be there."

"What of it? You can't be afraid of a sick person, and anyway, it will be best for you two to meet again in daylight. It was pretty rotten for you last night, but you've been through worse than that."

"She may accuse me again."

"That was the drug talking. She'd been swallowing something to swamp her sorrows."

Tess closed her fingers tightly over his sleeve. "I'm not a baby, Luke, nor a moron. It was bad enough at the log-house. One can't live through that type of experience more than once."

He stopped and gazed down at her, his lean face drawn into new lines of anxiety. "What do you know?" he asked quietly.

"That . . . Redding was the gun-runner who tried to poison me. Dave has always pretended that the gun-runner and Redding were two different men because he didn't want me to realize that he had killed a man."

"Dave didn't kill Redding—he wounded him. Redding took poison while he was in the clinic."

"Oh." It was half sigh and half shudder. Tess had gone white and was leaning against him.

"Tess." He spoke urgently, close to her ear. "You had no idea about this till last night, had you?"

"No. The woman's voice . . . I'd heard it before, at that house—but it was more lively then. It was she who made the man give me the coffee and turn me loose in the trees. Maria heard her, too. He didn't want to do it."

"Oh, my God!" He muttered it twice. "Look, Tess. We're going to the boat. If Avia's about, ignore her. Slip into your cabin and lock it."

Luke was suddenly active. He marched her the last few yards to the waterfront, and whistled up the taxi.

Ten minutes later it deposited them at the end of the jetty.

As Tess reached the deck Dave appeared.

"All right?" he asked quickly. "You're tired, Tess."

"Sure she is." Luke, conscious of Avia's approach, gave Tess a small dig in the back. "Go and have a cold wash and lie down." As she moved off he exchanged quick glances with Dave. "How about a short one to help the sun down?"

"Suits me."

"You, too, Mrs. Redding?"

Avia inserted an arm in Dave's. "A long one," she said languidly. "A very long one."

In the main cabin it was Luke who poured the drinks. His first intention had been to draw Dave aside for a lightning consultation, and thereafter to let him handle the situation. But Avia was sticking close, as she had no doubt done all day, and in spite of weakness, she had the air of a woman in fair control of herself. So Luke gave her a whisky-and-soda and pushed a similar drink across to Dave. There were no more chairs, so he perched uncomfortably on the edge of a bunk.

He lifted his drink. "Here's to the living . . . and the dead," and he took a sip.

"The toast was in very bad taste," said Avia.

"Merely a warning," he remarked. "I've been learning all about you, Avia. I'm rather curious as to one thing. Cast your mind back a bit. You never saw Tess while she was in that log-house, did you?"

Avia's whole face compressed and an excessive whiteness was visible each side of her nostrils. "I don't know what you're talking about. I had no knowledge of the house till Francis was dead. I've stated that under oath."

"I remember that, but it's rather odd. Because Tess saw you."

Dave sprang up. "What are you trying to do, Walt? Tess has said she saw only the two Portuguese and Redding?"

"Meeting Avia last night reminded her of an incident which occurred just before she was taken from the house. She told me about it less than an hour ago."

176

He paused. "Perhaps you will answer just one more question, Avia. When you persuaded your husband that the girl he had captured from the freight train was dangerous and would have to be put out of the way, were you aware that she was Dave's wife?"

If Luke had expended hours rehearsing for his effect it could not have been more shattering. Every drop of blood seemed driven from Dave's face as he watched the scarlet-clad, shaking creature in the canvas chair. For a full minute Luke feared he had overdone it. Then he heard Dave pull out a breath from the depths of his lungs and speak to the woman.

"You haven't answered, Avia!"

"Don't stare at me like that, Dave. I'm ill . . . you know I'm ill." Avia jerked up her glass and dashed half the whisky down her throat. "Yes . . . I did go to the house, but I was too terrified to admit it at the enquiry. I didn't see the girl, and if I had I wouldn't have known her. We . . . Francis was frantic because he had traced through a cheque-book that she had some connection with you. I had no inkling what the connection might be till we returned to Lokola, and Brigham let out that you were married. Then I . . . pieced all the happenings together." Hoarse with anger, she turned upon Luke. "If she told you she saw me she's lying. Francis would never let me be seen by anyone."

"Did I say that Tess saw you? I meant that she heard you, and last night recognized your voice."

By the aid of whisky Avia had regained some of her command. With creditable poise she rose to her feet.

"Seeing that you're only half-informed, I'll be gracious and give you the rest. It was I who pressed Francis to enter the gun racket. I wanted money—casks of it—because I was sick of being despised and living at the wrong end of the station; I'd lived that way all my life. I told you I had married a Belgian, but I only lived with him—"

"Call a taxi, Walt," said Dave sharply.

Avia lifted her shoulders. "Let him go. I'd just as soon only you heard it, Dave. Goodbye, Walt," she called after him.

"Come out on deck," Dave said grimly.

"No. When I walk out I'll do it alone, thanks." Avia's features went cold and still her lips hardly moved. "At Lokola I became ambitious. I was after enough money to make me free of Francis Redding, and I rather thought that you and I might make a go of it one day. Now that I've met that girl I can understand the coolness in you, which always piqued me before. She's nice, Dave. She hasn't been kicked around, like I was —"

"Shut up and go!"

"I haven't finished. Confession is necessary to a soul in torment. I heard an evangelist yell that once. Well, here's some more of mine. I didn't deceive myself when you were so kind to me in Fort Leppa. Obviously you felt bad because the man you had shot was my husband, and had been your friend, and you were determined to make the road easy for me. I got the impression that everything would come my way . . . if Francis died."

Curtly Dave replied, "You're already said too much."

"Perhaps, but it doesn't matter now. You've guessed, haven't you?"

"Yes. Each time you visited your husband in the clinic you begged him to take a doctored drink. You left the tablets in his bedside cupboard so that it would appear like suicide."

"Quite right. I did." Her heavy lids drooped, as if she were weary. "Though I did have hopes that the stuff wouldn't be detected, so that you would blame yourself for his death. Perhaps you can imagine the jolt I got when Brigham flapped around squawking that you had a wife?"

"You're trash . . . and crazy besides. Redding was decent enough till you fastened your claws into him. We've nothing more to say to each other. You'd better go."

Her teeth closed hard over her lower lip and when they released it a spot of blood oozed over the carmine. Dave lowered his gaze. Like this she was a pitiable object.

She squared her shoulders. "I ought to thank you for not handing me over to the authorities. If I were a man you'd have twisted my neck. I'm sorry I'm . . . not a man."

Dave didn't see her go; rather, he sensed the removal of her presence from the cabin. He drank down the whisky, and tried to relax his rigid muscles while he unlocked the medicine-case and sought through it for luminal. If Tess were given some hot milk and a couple of capsules right away she might sleep through till dawn. Armando could be sent ashore to round up the other two seamen and before daybreak the *Bondoa* could be well out and heading south. He'd be glad to have done with West Africa.

But Dave was reckoning without Avia's final gesture.

Mechanically, Tess had begun to follow Luke's advice. She bathed her face in cold water and shut herself into the cabin; but she did not lie down. She stood between the two blue-blanketed bunks and held clammy fingers to her pulsing temples.

The ventilator had been shut off and the air was stuffy and stagnant. The walls pressed in upon her as her skull seemed to be pressing upon her brain. Presently she tugged open the porthole. The sinking sun slanted in, hot and golden. The sea was flat and treacly pitted with flying fish. A launch chugged abeam of the *Bondoa;* Tess heard the raucous Portuguese pidgin common in these waters and guessed that a party of seamen were going ashore for the evening. Caged and stifled, she roamed the narrow cabin, and finally she unlocked the door and mounted the companionway.

The deck was deserted, but Luke was hurrying to the head of the jetty, a rangy-looking puppet at this distance. Tess followed him with her eyes till he disappeared behind a truckload of merchandise which had recently been unloaded from a vessel.

A cold, moist hand touched her bare arm, and in sudden terror she faced round to look into the haggard, hollow-eyed countenance of Avia Redding. Instinctively she recoiled.

Avia slowly shook her head; her red mouth widened into a long, crooked smile. Without speaking, she dragged up the gangway and for a moment she stood outlined against the sky, a vividly lonely figure. In a state of half-paralysis Tess watched her walk forward as though each step called for fresh physical effort. She

179

noticed that the woman had her head raised, and she had the frightful conviction that the dark eyes were closed. Avia was making straight for the edge of the stone-jetty.

Horrified, Tess watched the stumble and the headlong topple into the water. An instant later she screamed, and sprang from the side of the ship. She struck out towards the spot where Avia had disappeared and swam around till the dark head surfaced. Whatever happened she must keep her eye rigidly averted from the dead-white, dripping mask and the floating black hair.

She reached out and grabbed at Avia's waist, but was unprepared for the maniac force of the other woman's fist against her collar-bone.

"Get away, damn you!" Avia tugged herself free and let out hard with her foot. Her eyes glittered now, like smooth jet.

Tess felt the shoe in her rib, instinctively doubled with pain, and went under. She came up in time to see the lank tresses spread like seaweed over the oily water before they were drawn down into the black depths of the harbour.

A terrible sob wrenched her, and then another. Her mind and limbs had almost ceased to function. She was conscious of Dave's arm across her breast and of tears burning over her cold skin from the outer corners of her eyes as he swam with her to the boat. Luke leaned over to lend his strength as Dave lifted her aboard.

She lay on the deck, knees drawn up in an abandonment of convulsive weeping while Dave knelt at her side, pushing back strips of hair from her forehead and wincing as if her anguish were his.

"Tess . . . don't. You'll make yourself ill. It's all right now. There's nothing to be afraid of. Tess, please." He slipped an arm under her and held her trembling body.

Luke stooped beside him, offering a blanket. "She's had some breaks, lately. Shall I fetch a doctor?"

"It isn't necessary. It's nerves." Dave's voice sounded harsh and strange. "It's hell to listen to, but she's letting the tension out of her system. Put some towels in her cabin, will you, and prepare hot milk and whisky. I'll bring her along."

A beam of light filtered through the porthole. It lay in a bar of silver across the foot of the bunk and diffused enough radiance to awaken Tess. She remained still, while noises and a new day seeped into her consciousness. Memories crept back, distant and vague. Her hand rested on the bruised rib and her mind shied away from its implications.

Carefully Tess sat up and slipped undone the top button of her pyjama jacket for coolness. She lowered her feet to the floor and only then realized that the steady throbbing came from the engine. The *Bondoa* was at sea.

With caution she planted her feet and stood up. From here she could see the streaked grey water bouncing by and the thin dark line of the coast. The sun was coming up like a flight of flamingoes across a wash of lavender.

She heard steps on the companionway and snatched up her dressing-gown from the back of a chair. She was scarcely into it before the door opened and Dave came in carrying a tray. He smiled, drummed a belated tattoo on the inside of the door and placed the tray on the small, built-in dressing-table.

"You look better for the sleep," he said. "No head?"

"Nothing that fresh air won't dispel." She tied the belt of the wrap. "Where are we going?"

"To the next port."

"Have we been sailing long?"

"About seven hours."

She drank the tea he brought her, put down the cup and went nearer to the porthole. Her hair flew back in the breeze and a fine spray met her skin. The bones of her jaw and chin visibly sharpened, and she spoke almost inaudibly.

"Why do such horrors have to happen? There was no link at all between that woman and me, yet as long as I live she'll haunt me."

"She won't, Tess. There'll be too many other things, and soon you'll feel nothing but pity for a creature with a contorted outlook."

Her hands clenched in her pockets. "From the moment she touched me I knew she wanted to die. What made me dash into the harbour after her?"

"It was a natural reaction, though I wished to God you hadn't."

"I'm sorry I behaved so noisily after you hauled me out."

"So am I," he said. "I had to keep telling myself that a storm on top of such an incident was the best outlet, but I'll admit to being unnerved. You can't even cry without going the whole hog." He came behind her. "You see it all now, don't you, Tess? I'd always got along with Redding, and it shook me a bit when you described him as the man who made you drink the dope, but I had to get him just the same. I suspected that Avia knew more about the guns than she confessed to at the enquiry, but after Redding's death she wilted badly and I arranged for her to be taken to the coast. I'd crippled her husband in the first place, and I felt responsible for her. You didn't tell me you heard a woman's voice in that house."

"You questioned me at Dr. Greaves' on the evening of the day you found me. I told you all I remembered, and after that you always avoided discussion about it. Somehow, I didn't regard the woman as the man's wife. He must have been very much in love with her."

"The marriage was headed for trouble from the beginning, but no one foresaw such a sticky end to it." His voice lowered. "It's past, Tess, but we're still here."

Gently, he twisted her towards him. There was no arrogance about him, not even the usual amount of self-assurance. The events of the past day or two had left an imprint which Tess longed to obliterate.

"Tess, have you ever thought that if you'd married me when I asked you, none of these ghastly things would have happened? We'd have gone to Lokola for a visit and returned to our home at Zinto. By now we might even have been expecting a youngster."

She whitened to the lips. "It's cruel to talk that way."

"I don't mean to be cruel. More than anything I want you to understand my side of it." He dropped his hands from her shoulders and leaned back upon the end of the bunk. "From the day we met you had a profound influence upon me. For the first time in my life I was a victim of all those instincts which are supposed to be dying out. I wanted to protect you and cherish you, and I wanted you to belong to me. But you were independent and a spitfire, and just a bit highly strung, so that any clear-cut procedure I may have had in my mind needed to be flexible. Perhaps I'm to blame that it wasn't. I'll never be able to explain just how I felt those last days before I left Zinto—as if all heart and reason had been torn out of me, as if the most splendid thing in my whole existence had been dragged through slime."

"Dave," she whispered.

"That's what I meant that day at Badoun when I said you didn't understand me yet." He paused. "Back in Lokola, I did my best to view everything objectively. You were only twenty; how could you possibly realize that you stood for so much in my life? It was up to me to show you how deeply you had penetrated, and to give you time. I've told you why I didn't come for you, but I could never put into words the bitterness and hate which decided me to sink back into Lokola. I knew from experience that the tropics have a deadening effect on the emotions."

Her fingers were tightly entangled with her girdle, her eyes had gone huge, and extraordinarily dark.

"To a great extent," she said with difficulty, "the tropics succeeded, didn't they?"

"You've never been a man in love, so you can't appreciate the sensation of having your inmost being written off as worth a jade ring or a dilapidated store. We began all wrong, but it went too deep with me for that to matter much. What did matter was that we should belong together in every way as soon as possible." He breathed rather heavily. "Yes, the tropics helped me to slip into a consistently black mood, so that whenever I thought of you I could remind myself that you were no more to be trusted than the rest. I got into a peculiar state of mind in which I hadn't even the most primitive use for a woman, and I told myself that if I were to meet you again you'd affect me no more than the sight of a native woman passing the house."

"But when I did turn up it wasn't like that—was it?"

"No, it wasn't." He shifted his gaze from her face to the cream-painted wall behind her. "In almost your first breath you flipped a cheque at me and announced your intention of marrying Barnwell. After that I had to punish you as I'd been punished. It all appears foolish and unnecessary now, but I didn't know then that you'd clear off on a freight train and get yourself nearly murdered."

Tess gave a broken little sigh. "Ever since that happened you've hated me."

"No. I've only wished I could hate you." On a swift note of savagery, he demanded: "Why the hell didn't you marry me a year ago? Don't you see what a difference that year makes? I've been hating you, and you've let another man make love to you."

"No, Dave! It was because I couldn't allow that that I went to England. I would never have come to Lokola —I wouldn't be here with you, if I didn't love you."

He spoke more calmly, though the chiselled mouth was still compressed. "It's what we've lost that hurts," he said, and walked out.

What they'd lost. As Tess reached for a chair and sank into it, her brain reiterated the words. Only now was she beginning to appreciate the full depths of Dave's personality. How young and blind she had been at Zinto, how thoroughly unfledged; yet their love had been fresh and adventurous, and, for her, a wondrous melting of the bones at his touch, a strange sweet ecstasy of giving till she was drained dry. Maybe she had not entirely fathomed his mentality, but surely that would have come, in time?

They had lost nearly a year, a loss which Dave resented with disproportionate bitterness. He was upset over the business with Mrs. Redding; they both were. It was that which had brought their own affairs so precipitously into the open before either of them was quite ready for it.

She remembered the tenderness with which he had helped her out of her sodden garments last night, his repeated: "Don't cry so, darling. You'll make yourself ill," and the gentleness with which he had persuaded her to swallow luminal. He loved her, and how could anything be wrong if they were in love with each other?

A little wearily, she accomplished her toilet. She put on white linen shorts and a blue silk shirt, and used a trace of lipstick. The blue eyes which stared back from her mirror still had too much grief in their depths. Futilely, she wished that Dave had kept away from the cabin this morning. They both needed time in which to recover from yesterday's tragedy. They should have been wordless, but close, for a while—at least until it were possible to exchange a spontaneous smile.

Tess thrust shut a drawer in the dressing-chest, and slowly let herself out of the cabin. She mounted to the deck, answered the deck-hand's, *"Bom dia, senhora!"* and stood for a moment in the breeze which blew down the coast. The sky had the translucency of early morning; the horizon was screened by a wide, milky vapour; the sails belled with the pink of sun behind them, and the rigging creaked comfortingly.

The cook came along and told her that breakfast was ready in the main cabin, and soon she made her way there.

Dave was sitting in a chair beside a bunk, upon which an open deed-box spilled envelopes and loose papers. He looked up, nodded, and went on with his search.

"Isn't Luke about?" asked Tess.

"Luke," said Dave, "is still in Kanos. One of us had to stay and see the police, and he volunteered. He was nearly as worried over you as I was, and just as keen that you shouldn't wake up this morning to find the *Bondoa* still moored at the jetty. He won't hang on there any longer than necessary."

"Where are we picking him up?"

"We're not," he said. "When Walt's finished in Kanos he's going to make his way to Durham. I'll get in touch with him through the bank—we both use the same one."

"Oh." Tess drifted over to the table and rearranged a knife. "Is Luke definitely going to buy a native store?"

"That seems to be his idea."

Dave lit upon the envelope he had been seeking and set it aside. The rest of the papers were shovelled into the box and the lid was snapped down upon them. He came over and pulled out her chair.

"Let's eat," he said. "I detest cold eggs."

It was an almost silent meal, and neither had much appetite. Armando arched his brows sorrowfully as he lifted the cover from the metal dish before transferring it to his tray, and clearing the rest of the table.

Tess had moved to the chair. She was sitting close to the bunk which held the deed-box and, unintentionally, she read the scribbled words on the foolscape envelope which lay beside it.

Dave said: "Yes, it's my birth certificate. I'd like to have yours, too."

"Mine? What for?"

"It'll be less trouble to get a licence if I can produce them both at once. We'll be tying up at a fairly large mission settlement before lunch, and lots of these missionaries have the power to perform the ceremony right away."

Tess had nothing to say.

Dave sat on the edge of the bunk, at her side. "In Kanos, before Mrs. Redding crossed our path," he said quietly, "I'd arranged with Walt that we should part at the next stop. I believe he realized that I had to have you to myself. He and I talked over the future and decided that Natal would be a good place to settle. I suggested that he inspect all the larger farms that might be for sale, and if there were one with a store on the property, he should at once take an option and let me know."

"Why did you leave me out of the conference?"

"Too much depended on you. Everything was left fluid because a farm would be no good to me if you weren't there."

"But I'm going to be there."

He nodded, his manner still dry and unemotional. "We'll keep the boat, too—sail her round to the nearest coastal town and use her when we need a change from farming."

She smiled, rather tremulously. "Dave, have you ever heard of a place called Hermanus?"

"No. Where is it?"

"On the Coast at the Cape. There's wonderful rock fishing and bathing, and profusions of wild flowers. We can rent a bungalow overlooking the sea. Will you . . . can we live there till Luke hits upon a proposition?"

"If you like."

With some of her former impulsiveness she leaned over and caught his hand. "Please be happy, Dave. We have to make up for that year. I'll never forget how you feel about it, and I'll try so hard to erase it for you. I'll do whatever you wish—always."

He smiled slightly. "Don't be too rash with your promises—and don't worry about me. I've known for a long time that I love you more than you love me, but I don't intend it always to be so."

So that was it! Tess released his hand and lay back, quite stunned for a second. Again it was humiliation, of a kind, which made a stranger of him. But this time he was going to submit to it rather than lose her. Tess wanted to cry out that there was no need for him to feel let down, almost defeated, in finally acknowledging how much she meant to him. But she was checked by a swift recollection. Hadn't Dave been kinder to Mariella in the long run than she had to Martin? He had not bolstered the girl's hope with half-promises, or allowed her private affairs to impinge upon his own—because already he had been falling in love with Tess. She could not say the same for herself, with Martin.

Dimly, it came to her that back in Zinto, Dave's love had been definitely greater than her own; ruthless, consuming and one-track. She had been too young in such matters to comprehend its magnitude. Suffering, not so much one's own as that of the beloved, made one wise. How could she convince him that at last she perceived how harrowing pain had prompted his cruelty, at last she was fit to be loved as he loved her? It would take months, possibly years, of constant proof. She was equal to it, of course, but what a waste it was going to be, what an appalling, heart-wrenching waste.

Dave had stood up, and was looking down at her. Her uplifted face mirrored the sweetness and poignancy of her thoughts, her eyes were lustrous with an unbearable yearning. He drew a sharp breath and pulled her up into his arms.

His mouth warm against her cheek, he said thickly, "This is worth it, Tess . . . this is worth the agony of the last year."

Golden Harlequin $1.95 per vol.

Each Volume Contains 3 Complete Harlequin Romances

☐ Volume 10

FOUR ROADS TO WINDRUSH by Susan Barrie (No. 687)
Lindsay wasn't sure she could endure this much longer, after all, this "house" where she was now employed, was once her own home. Old Mr. Martingale had been a delight to work for, then the new owner came — a tyrant, a martinet — a brute.

SURGEON FOR TONIGHT by Elizabeth Houghton (No. 724)
Jan was about to enter a marriage which would salve her conscience, but break her heart. Dr. Ritchie, a man who found little time for play, and even less for women, had the power to spare her this heartbreak, if only he could become "human" enough, and in time . . . .

THE WILD LAND by Isobel Chace (No. 821)
The little town of Les Saintes de la Mer. The annual gathering of gypsies from all over Europe. When Emma was summoned to France to visit her grandmother, she was not prepared for all this excitement, and even less prepared for Charles Rideau!

☐ Volume 11

NURSE OF ALL WORK by Jane Arbor (No. 690)
When everyone around her seemed to shun her, there was Glen Fraser, the new Welfare Officer. Nurse Nightingale was grateful to him, it would indeed have been so easy to love him, but for the unsuperable barrier which stood between them . . . .

HOUSE OF THE SHINING TIDE by Essie Summers (No. 724)
Lorette — a perfect nuisance to her stepsister, was finally going to be off Judith's hands, so, to keep Lorette's engagement together, Judith did everything possible. Ironically, it was through the troublesome Lorette that Judith herself found the key to a lasting happiness.

ALL I ASK by Anne Weale (No. 830)
To heal a broken heart, Francesca decided she must "get away". Wisely, she chose the remote Andorra, in the heart of the Pyrenees. Was it equally as wise however, for her to remain in the orbit of the attractive Nicholas de Vega.

Golden Harlequin $1.95 per vol.
Each Volume Contains 3 Complete Harlequin Romances

☐ ## Volume 16

LOVE HIM OR LEAVE HIM by Mary Burchell   (No. 616)
In anger — he fired her, later to find that he desperately needed her help. Anne volunteered, and what began as a generous gesture, developed into a situation full of pitfalls, chiefly in the form of his jealous fiancee!

DOCTOR'S ORDERS by Eleanor Farnes   (No. 722)
It was incredible — like a dream. Here she was, in Switzerland, in a world of beauty, luxury and leisure. The events which took place before this lovely fresh Swiss Summer drew to its happy close, were no dream, for Diana, this would last forever . . . .

PORTRAIT OF SUSAN by Rosalind Brett   (No. 783)
Managing Willowfield Farm in Rhodesia had made Susan and Paul supremely happy. Then, the owner, David Forrest returned. For her brother's sake, Susan had tolerated his iron-hard selfishness, but how long could her endurance last . . . .

☐ ## Volume 22

THE SONG AND THE SEA by Isobel Chace   (No. 725)
When Charlotte came from New Zealand to Europe to have her voice trained, she did not expect to find her father whom she thought dead, nor to be diving in the Red Sea with him, a charming marine biologist and a beautiful French girl.

CITY OF PALMS by Pamela Kent   (No. 791)
On the plane from Paris to Bagdad, Susan had noticed the handsome stranger, with a certain air of aloofness about him. In the emergency which followed, his "aloofness" vanished and he came to her aid, and yet again, in the firghtening wildnerness of the desert . . . .

QUEEN'S NURSE by Jane Arbor   (No. 524)
"He has the power to get what he wants", Jess thought bitterly, about this complete stranger. Later, taking up her first "district" as "Queen's Nurse", to her astonishment, she now hoped that this "power" would be directed towards herself!

Golden Harlequin $1.95 per vol.

Each Volume Contains 3 Complete Harlequin Romances